Love's No Joke

Other Bella Books by Cheri Ritz

Vacation People
Let The Beat Drop

About the Author

Cheri Ritz loves a good romance, so writing some happily ever after to share with the world is a dream come true! She enjoys attending her sons' many activities, brushing up on pop culture trivia, and spending cozy weekends marathoning TV shows. She lives in a suburb of Pittsburgh, Pennsylvania with her wife, three sons, and the Sweetest Cat in the World.

Love's No Joke

Cheri Ritz

BELLA
BOOKS
2021

Bella Books, Inc.
P.O. Box 10543
Tallahassee, FL 32302

Printed in the United States of America on acid-free paper.

First Bella Books Edition 2021

Editor: Ann Roberts
Cover Designer: Heather Honeywell

ISBN: 978-1-64247-200-4

Acknowledgments

As always, I must begin with a great big heartfelt thank you to Jessica and Linda Hill and all the fine folks at Bella Books. You are supportive, and wonderful, and I appreciate all the magic you do to make our stories happen. Thank you also to my editor Ann Roberts. Your guidance and wisdom made this book shine. You have a gift, and I'm so, so grateful that you've shared it with me.

Writing can be a solitary experience, so I remain especially grateful for my Bella author family, my author friends, and the lesfic community. I also want to thank my friends at Lesbian Story Hour—spending time with our group always sparks my creativity and fires me up to get pen on paper.

I am blessed to have the best, most supportive sisters on the planet, Shelly, Stacey, and Jaymie. Thank you for all the words of encouragement, kicks in the butt, cheers, jokes and heart emojis. I don't have the words to express how much it means to me to have you in my life.

To my boys, you bring so much joy to my life. Thank you just for being you.

I couldn't do any of this without the continuous support of my wife. I never would have dared write a book about a comedian without my favorite funny woman by my side. You've been along for the ride since the Lez Vegas series was just a few lines and scribbled notes in a funky purple notebook. What a ride it has been! Jaime, you are my inspiration and my heart. Thank you.

To my wife Jaime—my favorite person to laugh with.

CHAPTER ONE

"Let's face it, Jenkins is losing his touch." Mara Antonini crossed her arms and hitched her hip up onto the corner of her boss's desk, settling in. She would not be moved until she'd been heard. "He's a professional comedian who has a chicken crossed the road joke in his act, AND he managed to give it a homophobic twist. Then tonight he totally lashed out at that woman in the audience."

"Hey," Ricky Jenkins said with a frown. "She was heckling me, I responded. It's all part of the magical Las Vegas experience."

"You asked her if she was 'on the rag.' It's not nineteen eighty-six." She looked to Jerry, their boss, for backup, but he just sat there, his expression unimpressed, as if he was equally annoyed by Mara as he was his rogue headliner. "Who the hell even still says shit like that? It's time for the Rothmoor to enter the twenty-first century. Yes, Las Vegas is a magical place. Everybody has a dream here, but nobody's dream includes enduring hate speech at a comedy club."

Mara's dream was to secure the headliner slot for the night shows at Laffmoor, the comedy club at the Rothmoor Tower Casino. At least that was the short-term dream, with hopes that it would be a stepping-stone to a solid career in the comedy world. She had been doing the afternoon show regularly with a few warm-up slots in the evening for over a year, but as her thirtieth birthday had come and gone, she realized she needed to get her ass in gear and her career on track. She was nothing if not a work in progress, but actual progress hadn't reared its elusive head in a long while. Mara was due to catch a break, and she'd be damned if some throwback blowhard whose act revolved around insults and snickering at others was going to be the thing that stood in her way.

"Oh." Ricky swatted a big, meaty hand through the air dismissively. "Here we go with the dyke drama."

"Okay, no." Mara hopped off the desk and pointed a finger until she was close enough to poke him right in the beefy middle of his faded black T-shirt. "*I* can say dyke. *You* can't say dyke. This is exactly what I'm talking about. It's not edgy and it's not funny. It's offensive. This stuff doesn't fly anymore. Remind me again, when were you born? Before or just slightly after fire was invented?"

"You can call me a caveman, but I can't call you a dyke? *That's* offensive."

"Sure," she nodded. She waited a beat, the perfect comedic timing she was known for. "It's offensive to cavemen."

Ricky scowled. "You know what, Mara? You better watch your—"

"Enough!" Jerry finally spoke up. "You've both said enough for one night. Ricky, get out of here. We'll discuss the heckling issue later."

"Fine by me. I don't need to hear anymore from this bitch. We'll talk business tomorrow. Just us men." He slammed the office door as he left.

"And he thinks I bring the drama?" Mara stomped her foot in frustration. "That man is misogynistic and homophobic, and he smells like he took a swim in a vat of cheap cologne."

"That is all accurate," Jerry said rubbing his temples. "But he's also our headliner and under contract. He might be a jerk but he's the Laffmoor's jerk."

"Wonderful." She dropped into the chair opposite Jerry. "That could be the Laffmoor's new slogan. Let's get T-shirts made."

"Mara, come on. Be reasonable here. The guy made some bad choices on stage. So what? The show must go on."

"He continually makes bad choices on stage, and you allowing him do it night after night is part of the problem."

"I already said I'd talk to him about the incident." Jerry wasn't a big man like Ricky, but he had a gruff voice. It commanded attention and respect. "So, are you satisfied?"

"No. But I'm glad you asked." She leaned back in the chair and crossed her legs. She was not satisfied and she finally had the opportunity to say something about it. "Last week when Ricky flaked on his set, you brought in an outsider to cover for him instead of bumping me up to headliner for the night. I think that was crap. You should be calling me first when something like that happens."

Jerry blew out a sigh. "It was nothing against you. There's not a comedy club on the strip that has a woman headliner. Maybe a guest spot, but not a resident. That's just the way it is."

"Well, it's not the way it has to be. This is our chance to be trailblazers. It could set the Laffmoor apart. Come on, Jerry. Stand up for women everywhere. One small step for womankind, you know?"

"I hear you. Woman power. Pink pussy hats. I'll take that under advisement." He wasn't listening to her. He was dismissing her.

Mara stood but she wasn't ready to exit the office quite yet. "I'm serious, Jerry. If Ricky isn't available to do the show, I should be your first call. I deserve that."

"Mara," He growled and ran a hand through his ash-colored hair. Mara hoped his receding hairline could take the stress. "It's late and I still have shit to do before I can get out of here. I'll think about it, but that's the best I can give you."

"I gotta say, Jerry, I don't have a ton of faith in your thinking." It was out of her mouth before she remembered finesse was a crucial part of any negotiation.

"Mara." It was a bark of warning. The discussion was over.

"Fine." She slammed the door on her way out. If it worked for Ricky, maybe it would work for her too.

Her jaw clenched tight as she marched through the casino. That son-of-a-bitch. "I'll think about it" meant a whole hell of a lot of nothing, and they both knew it. The chime of an incoming text on her phone interrupted her annoyed thoughts and gave her angst a moment of reprieve.

Looking forward to coming next weekend.

Yeah you will! Mara smiled and hit send.

"What are you smiling like that for?" Penny Rothmoor was the picture of professionalism in her tailored black suit and turquoise blouse, her blond hair neatly pulled into a bun at the nape of her neck as she fell into step next to Mara. "Who were you texting?"

Mara wiggled her phone back into her back pocket. Her attire for the evening—ripped jeans, chunky black leather boots, and a tight-fitting black V-neck T-shirt was a stark contrast to her best friend's. "What?" she blinked innocently, not interested in texting and telling. "No one."

"No one my ass. I know that look. That patented 'Mara on the prowl' look." Penny had started out as Assistant to the General Manager at her family's casino after she graduated from college, and she'd worked her way up to her current position as Executive Manager. She and Mara had been best friends since college. They had been in tune like sisters for a decade. There was no hiding from each other when it came to stuff like that. "It's a chick you're texting. Give it up. Who?"

"It was Kat. You know. From New York."

"Ah! The Booty Call Chef." Penny's eyes lit up with recognition and she nodded sagely.

"I mean, we're friends. And she's going to be in town next week. So we'll probably get together." It was no big deal.

"For a booty call."

"Would you stop saying that?" Mara pulled a face at her, but Penny was right. Kat worked at a restaurant in New York City with a sister location in another casino on the strip. They met one day after Kat had come to the show at the Laffmoor, and they immediately hit it off. Kat flew into Vegas once every couple of months to oversee things at the restaurant, and they always tried to see each other, but neither was interested in a long-distance relationship. Instead they kept in touch and settled on a "friends with benefits" kind of thing.

"You and your women," Penny sighed. "Don't you ever want to settle down?"

There it was, the million-dollar question Mara's friends had asked her again and again. All this time the answer hadn't changed. She was much too busy getting her career in gear to get tied down in a relationship.

"Sure," Mara shrugged. "Someday."

"Someday, someday," Penny singsonged with an eye roll, indicating she didn't believe her best friend in the least. "It's the same old story with you, Mara."

"Give me a break," Mara sighed. "It's been a long night. I just came from Jerry's office after catching Ricky Jenkins at the nine o'clock show."

It was Penny's turn to sigh. "Yes, I fielded a few complaints on that exact subject tonight."

"Then you know! I can't believe he went after that woman tonight. What the hell is he thinking?"

"My guess is, he's not." Penny shook her head. "Listen, Mara, you know I love you, but I can't go down this road with you. I'm your friend, but I'm a manager here too. I can't discuss another employee with you. It's not right."

"Yeah, I know. It's just so damn frustrating."

Penny took Mara's hand and gave it a squeeze. Silent support. "My shift is over. You ready to call it a night? It's almost midnight, and we promised Frankie we would be at the café in the morning. I need my beauty sleep."

Mara understood that Penny couldn't talk through the Laffmoor situation with her, but she still needed to find some way to unwind after the scene in Jerry's office. She glanced over at the blackjack table and caught the eye of a sexy brunette. She winked, earning a coy smile in response. She could help Mara work off a little stress. "I don't know. I'm thinking about trying my luck with a hand or two of blackjack."

Penny's gaze settled on the woman. Her eyes registered understanding. "You spread yourself too thin," she scolded with a frown. "It's late. Go home and be there for Frankie tomorrow."

"What is this project of Frankie's anyway?"

"She didn't say, but she was very excited." Penny put her hands on her hips, an authoritative stance that worked very well while managing her employees, but in all their years of friendship, it had never worked on Mara.

"Frankie's always very excited."

"Be nice." Penny hugged her best friend and gave her a peck on the cheek. "And be good tonight. See you in the morning."

"Please, I'm always good." Mara winked and headed off to the bar.

As they had promised, bright and early the next morning Penny and Mara walked into Café Gato, the local coffee shop conveniently connected to the animal shelter. They were both greeted with enthusiastic hugs from a very bubbly and possibly over-caffeinated Frankie Malone. Mara was still recovering from a nearly sleepless night of mattress dancing with the hot blackjack player and was not amused by the high-energy welcome. Early morning meetings were the pits.

"Come in, you two! I saved us the table over by the window and Singe is lounging on the cushion there." Frankie gestured happily toward the most coveted table in the joint with sunlight streaming in the window and an air-conditioning vent overhead. "I'll bring you over some coffee."

Singe—a big, fat orange cat—was Mara's favorite cat at the café, and Frankie Malone was her favorite ex-girlfriend. Actually, she was the only ex Mara even spoke to. Usually that shit was too messy, but they had been together for less than two months when it was mutually determined they made better friends than lovers and had parted on good terms. That was how their whole friend circle had started, and they were still going strong in spite of the uncoupling.

"What do you think this is about?" Penny whispered as she hung her designer handbag on the metal clip she had attached to the table.

"Maybe she wants us to adopt Singe. Look at this baby!" Mara reached over to the window seat and rubbed the lounging cat's furry beige belly.

"That *baby* is a giant. He's gotta be twenty pounds. And if that's what she wants, it's too bad. Neither of us can keep pets in our suites at the casino. You know that."

"Oh, you and your rules." Mara's mouth twisted into a tight-lipped grimace at her best friend's no-nonsense attitude. "You've been really grumpy this week, you know that?"

"They're not my rules. I don't make them." Penny shook out the napkin from her place setting and primly set it on her lap. "And of course I'm grumpy. I'm stressed about work and I miss my girlfriend. I don't have my person here to talk things through with."

Penny and her girlfriend Lauren were in a long-distance relationship for the time being, flying back and forth between Vegas and Chicago when their schedules allowed until Lauren moved there permanently in a couple more months.

"You can talk to me about stuff."

"I can talk to you about stuff, but not about work," Penny said. "When it comes to work stuff, especially about the Laffmoor, you're my employee. What I said last night works both ways. There are lines we can't cross."

"Sure. But the cat thing," Mara challenged. "Admit you're just being a party pooper."

"Am not!"

"What party are you pooping now?" Frankie asked, setting mismatched colorful coffee cups in front of each of the women before joining them.

"See?" Mara shrugged at Penny. She enjoyed the aroma of the hot coffee before adding cream and an unhealthy amount of sugar. Besides the charm of visiting the cats, the Café really did serve a good cup of joe, keeping patrons coming back for more. "I cannot wait for Lauren to come back into town so you can chill out again."

"We were merely admiring Singe," Penny explained.

"Oh!" Frankie's chocolate brown eyes lit up. Of course she was well aware of the Rothmoor's rules, but that didn't mean she wouldn't take a chance to give her furry friend a forever home. "Do you want to take him home with you? Singe would make a great companion. He could keep you company while Lauren is in Chicago."

Penny smiled kindly. "Thanks, but no thanks."

"So what's your big news?" Mara asked. The sooner they got through the announcement, the sooner she could get back to bed. A mid-morning nap sounded like a damn good idea.

"You know how the animal shelter is always trying to come up with good fundraisers? I pitched an idea last week that the board said I could run with." She paused to blow across the surface of her hot coffee. "I'm going to host a basket auction/comedy night here at the Café. All proceeds will go to the animal shelter."

Frankie had started hanging out at the cafe years before when she started working at the animal shelter, before Mara even lived in Las Vegas. Café Gato's partnership with the shelter next door helped the business grow into the success it had become. The sweet older couple who owned the café, Zig and Maeve, had worked out an arrangement where Frankie brought in some of the cats from the shelter for the patrons to enjoy a little cat therapy while they consumed their coffee and muffins. Sometimes there was a pet-love connection and a cat got adopted out of the deal. It also earned Frankie free reign at the café. A win-win.

Mara nodded. "That sounds fun."

"Agreed. It's a great idea," Penny chimed in.

"I'm glad you think so, Penny." Frankie pulled her full-out big, beaming smile. "I was hoping the Rothmoor would be one of the main sponsors." Then she turned the high-wattage grin to her ex-girlfriend. "And Mara, you would make a really great emcee. What do you say?"

"I say yes." Any chance to get her name out there was a good one, and publicity was the best way to get ahead in the entertainment business.

"Penny?"

"I'll have to run it by our people, just as a formality of course, but unofficially I'd say we're in."

"Thank you, thank you, thank you!" Frankie clapped her hands and stomped her feet under the table, making the springy curls on the top of her head bob and hop. Enthusiasm could have been her middle name. It was cute and charming and had totally overwhelmed Mara when they were together as a couple. "And I'm going to take the two of you out to dinner to show my appreciation."

"Not the five-dollar buffet, Frankie." Mara wrinkled her nose. Frankie had dragged the group to her favorite "cheap eats" spot on the strip more times than Mara cared to admit.

"What?" Frankie pouted. "They have the biggest selection of vegetarian dishes on the strip and still plenty of meat for you carnivore-types."

"Well, count this carnivore-type out, although I do love being compared to a dinosaur," Penny said. She had plopped her large, leather, designer handbag on her lap and dug through it, avoiding eye contact with Frankie. "I have a thing Grandad wants me to attend. There's no getting out of it."

Lies. Clearly all lies, Mara thought. But there was no use calling her out on it. Until Lauren came back she would have to cut Penny a little slack. That's what best friends did. Mara tipped her head to the side, regarding Frankie with a grin. "Guess it's just you and me, kiddo."

CHAPTER TWO

Victoria McHenry plopped down on the corner of her bed and toed off her clogs, exhausted after an eight-hour shift on her feet at Sunset General Hospital. The Emergency Room had been nonstop action per usual, and she was glad to be leaving the brutal shift behind. She was not in the most generous mood, a fact that was coming through loud and clear in her phone call with her sister, Maddie. "No, no, no. I am begging you. Do not ask me to do this."

"Please, Vicki?" Maddie whined.

Victoria could picture her sister's beautiful, perfectly made up face all scrunched and pouty. Using Victoria's old high school nickname wasn't helping her cause. "Don't call me that." It was Victoria or Vic. Never Vicki. No one could get away with that. At this point in her life, only her little sister still tried. "You know I hate these kinds of things. That's why I went out and carved out my own career path instead of sliding comfortably into the family business. You're the golden girl of the family. Not me."

"But Daddy said I have to be there. And I'm smack in the middle of this ski trip. I'm having a really good time. All my friends are here and I don't want to leave. It would be rude."

Victoria cringed at her sister's use of "daddy." There was no good reason for a twenty-two-year-old woman to say that. Maddie played the spoiled socialite role so well. Not even a full year out of college and her life was ballgowns, overpriced lattes, and apparently, two-week ski trips with her besties. They most likely weren't even skiing. They were probably sleeping until noon, flirting with guys in the lodge during happy hour, and then clubbing all night. So why should Victoria take time out of her busy schedule to attend a meeting for some fundraiser her father wanted to join. Fundraisers and galas were basically Maddie's whole job. Nice work if you were into that sort of thing but Victoria most definitely was not.

"Maddie, this is your job. It trumps ski lodge shenanigans. You're not in school anymore. Stay for the weekend then come home." Victoria sighed reaching the end of her patience for the conversation as well as Maddie's attitude.

"I just need you to attend this one meeting for me Monday morning. Take some notes. I'll be back at the end of the week to handle it from there," Maddie said sweetly, something that always worked on men, not so much on older sisters.

"Ugh."

"Hey, I didn't give you shit when you asked me to watch your cat while you went on vacation. I just did the favor you asked. In fact, you even said you owed me one."

Victoria rolled her eyes so hard she was certain her sister could hear it through the phone. Like serious, Liz-Lemon-Masterpiece-strength eye roll. "First of all, that *vacation* was a business trip. I was taking continuing education classes. Secondly, you and your friends hung out at my house the whole weekend like it was some kind of sorority sleepover, eating everything in my fridge and abusing my Netflix account. I'm pretty sure I was doing you a favor there." But in spite of the strength of her words, she was weakening. Maddie had taken care of Buddy for that weekend and she had done it with no argument. She owed her for that. She paced across her living room. To give in or not?

"Please," Maddie pleaded, in full-on pout voice once again. "All I need you to do is go to this one meeting. Then you can wash your hands of it. Besides, this 'all work no play' lifestyle you're rocking is making you grumpy. You should let your hair down. Have a little fun. Get out there and meet someone."

It sounded like a bad cheer: *let your hair down/have a little fun/get out there and meet someone!* Visions of shaking pompoms, big hair and skimpy cheerleader outfits crossed Victoria's mind. It was true, she hadn't really dated anyone since her ex, Nadia, suddenly up and left her blindsided and heartbroken after almost three years together. That was over a year ago. Victoria had bounced back by focusing on her career, keeping busy and taking on an, "I'm doing me" attitude. She had Buddy to keep her company and give snuggles at home, and the two of them were doing just fine. As a bonus, she didn't have to deal with the drama of the lesbian dating scene. That was one thing she surely didn't miss, but she didn't need a lecture on it, especially not from Maddie, who wasn't exactly the picture of relationship expertise. Maddie was still in the live-in-the-moment phase of dating. She cast a pretty wide net, then threw back any catches with a low net worth or bad hair.

"I'm doing okay on my own. I don't need a 'someone' to make me complete."

"Oh, please. I'm not talking about making you complete. I'm talking about having a good time for a change. Do I need to remind you about grandmother's upcoming party? Are you really going to attend without a date and deal with mother's endless attempts at setting you straight?"

Maddie's superior tone was grating. "Setting me straight. That's very funny." Victoria wasn't laughing.

"I'm serious. Remember what happened last New Year's Eve?"

Victoria doubted she would ever purge the memory of that night from her mind. Fresh from her breakup with Nadia, she had attended her parents' annual New Year's Eve affair solo. Her mother introduced her to a seemingly endless stream of men by their full birth name as if they were royalty. Michael

Vincent Patton, David Spencer Wallace. She had never met so many two-syllable, three-name people in her life. Hardly princes or lords, they were either casino heirs or casino adjacent—restaurant moguls, talent managers, Vegas mob. Victoria had spent the whole night nodding politely at boring conversation and declining offers to "get outta here and go somewhere we can talk." No thank you.

Victoria had passed on attending the New Year's gala the following year, as well as most every other family event that had popped up since. But she didn't want to miss the celebration of Grandmother Siobhan's ninetieth birthday, and that meant facing her mother's ill-advised matchmaking attempts.

"Crap." She blew out her breath. "I need a date."

"You need a date," Maddie confirmed. "So get out there and meet someone. God, what would you do without me?"

Victoria had a couple of guesses, like stay the hell away from the Emerald Isle Casino, but she kept that to herself. Maddie had a point. She wasn't going to meet anyone if she never went out. There was always online dating, but how did you know who was really on the other end of that Internet connection? Vegas was nuts enough without wading through catfish on the Internet. Getting involved with a project would at least give her the chance to see who was out there in the world.

"Fine, I'll go to the meeting."

"Yay! Thank you!" Maddie squealed, and Victoria swore she could hear the high-fiving of many well-manicured hands through the chalet. "And don't forget to take notes."

"Forget to take notes? Have you met me?" Victoria laughed. "Just make sure you get your ass back here by the end of the week."

"I will. I promise." Maddie made a kissy noise before clicking off the call.

Victoria sighed and tossed her phone onto the bed. One conversation with Maddie and suddenly she was spending her day off with the stuffy high society fundraising set. What had she gotten herself into?

CHAPTER THREE

In Mara's dream the toaster was playing "Fly Like an Eagle" and that seemed perfectly logical. Classic rock made the appliance much cooler and she bobbed her head in approval. Ensconced in the cozy dreamscape, she didn't mind a repeat performance of the song as she opened the fridge and ogled the three-tiered birthday cake filling it up. What an odd, yet beautiful item to find in your refrigerator. Red, yellow and blue stage lights beamed around the kitchen as Mara reached for a slice of the sugary treat.

Her phone's ring tone pulled her awake. The rock 'n' roll kitchen faded away as she came to her senses. The text tone was chirping too. She pawed at the bedside table until she felt the phone under her hand.

Frankie had texted the same message over and over. *HELP. I THINK I'VE BEEN POISONED.*

The damn five-dollar buffet. How long had Frankie been trying to reach her? Mara dialed Frankie's number and didn't even wait for her to say anything when the call connected. "Frankie, are you all right? What happened?"

"I'm sick. It's...bad." The way Frankie's voice echoed indicated she was in a small space, most likely her apartment bathroom.

"Honey, you need to get some fluids. Do you have any Sports Ade? You want me to bring you some?" Mara rubbed her eyes, still trying to wake up, trying to focus on helping her friend.

The question was met with retching and the sound of Frankie's stomach emptying into the toilet.

"That didn't sound good," Mara groaned.

"Can't...keep...anything...down." Frankie sounded weak and her words were muffled. She probably had her head resting on the toilet seat. Mara's stomach gave a sympathetic flop picturing it. After Frankie caught her breath she said, "And I'm sweaty as fuck. Please, Mara, I need you to take me to the hospital. I think I'm dying."

Mara rolled her eyes. "You're not dying." Although if Frankie used the f-word, she must have been in rough shape. Rarely did she cuss. Food poisoning would pass, right? If that was really what this was. Maybe Frankie did need medical attention.

"Please come." Frankie sounded completely pathetic and weak, not a trace of her usual bubbly self to be found.

"I'll be there in a few," Mara promised before clicking off the call. She briefly considered calling Penny for reinforcements, but the last thing she needed was an earful about eating at the five-dollar buffet. It would have to be a solo rescue mission.

"This is fucking insane," Mara said.

They had been sitting in the emergency waiting room area for nearly an hour. Although Frankie hadn't vomited since they'd arrived, she still had a distinct yellowish-green tinge to her complexion. Mara's favorite gym shoes had been puked on in the parking lot of Frankie's apartment building, and between that and the way she had supported Frankie's sweaty body with her shoulder from the car into the hospital, she figured she was probably not at her fragrant best. No wonder the other hospital patrons had given them plenty of personal space—not a soul sat in the hard, plastic orange chairs immediately surrounding them. She glanced at Frankie clutching her white airsickness bag and couldn't blame them. Mara closed her eyes, took a deep breath through her mouth to avoid smelling her own stench, and promised herself the hottest, most soothing germ-killing shower ever the very second she returned home.

Frankie shifted in her seat and moaned. Instinctively Mara tucked her feet under her chair and out of any potential danger zone for projectile vomit.

"That's it. I'm gonna go see how the hell much longer this is going to take." Mara stood and turned toward the admissions window, giving the evil eye to the tired looking woman working there. The woman seemed much more engrossed with something on her phone than with the condition of the ailing and injured around her.

But before Mara could march herself over to demand action, a harried, yet kind voice from the door to the triage area called Frankie's name.

"Here! She's right here," Mara replied, waving a hand in the air to draw her attention. No way would they miss their turn and get moved to the end of the list again. *Not today, ma'am!* She grabbed Frankie by the wrists and pulled her to her feet, making a mental note to slather on hand sanitizer at the first opportunity. And maybe burn all the clothes she was wearing.

"Take it easy," Frankie winced as Mara dragged her to the doorway. "I'm dying here."

"You're not dying," Mara scolded, her patience reaching its end. The stress of worrying about her friend and then the prolonged wait time was wearing on her. "Now, come on and let the nice lady…" She trailed off as the nurse waiting for them looked up from her clipboard and locked her emerald eyes on Mara.

The smart-ass comment Mara was about to make dissipated as she got a good look at the beautiful woman standing before her. Slim build, ginger hair, chin cocked confidently in the air. A tingle ran up Mara's spine at the intensity of the nurse's gaze. Was it mutual interest? The nurse had full lips that begged to be kissed and a smattering of freckles that gave her just enough "girl next door" value to make it seem like earning that kiss could be a challenge. Mara loved a challenge, almost as much as she loved kissing a gorgeous woman.

"So what do we have here?" the nurse asked, her gaze flicking over to Frankie in her ill state. Then her expression softened as they approached. Her reddish hair was pulled back in a ponytail, but a few curly tendrils had fallen from it, framing her face. What was it about a woman in scrubs that made Mara's pulse race?

"Hi, I'm Mara." Turning on her million-dollar, on-stage smile, she released her grasp on Frankie. "And you are?"

"Victoria." Her lips curved into a shy grin as she tipped her head toward her official hospital badge—a cute, coy, almost flirty move. Was the nurse playing along?

"Hello?" Frankie whined from behind Mara, giving a weak little wave with her fingertips. "I've been poisoned and I'm dying."

"You're not dying," Victoria and Mara said at the same time, but as Mara started to laugh, the nurse slid right back into business mode, that sweet, coy smile gone without a trace and their connection severed.

"Nonetheless, we'll get you checked out." Victoria gave a stiff nod. "Follow me right back here."

"I'm sick as a dog and you're mackin' on the ER nurse?" Frankie angry-whispered to Mara as they made their way down the sterile, white hallway. "Thanks a lot."

"Hey, one of us may as well have a good morning," Mara teased.

Nurse Victoria led them into the small room and Mara took Frankie's arm and gingerly boosted her onto the paper-covered examining table. The thin paper crinkled as Frankie wiggled into a comfortable position.

"So tell me what happened," Victoria said, strapping the blood pressure cuff to Frankie's arm. She moved so swiftly that she was about three pumps in before Frankie answered.

Frankie continued to clutch her airsick bag like a security blanket. "I think I have food poisoning."

"We went to the five-dollar buffet for dinner," Mara explained with a slight cringe, anticipating the nurse's reaction.

"The five-dollar buffet?" Victoria scrunched up her face like Penny had the day before and shot Mara a disgusted look over her shoulder.

"I know, right? But Frankie likes the vegetarian selections there." Mara shook her head at the irony of it all. "Can you believe it? My meal was still mooing and she gets the food poisoning."

"This was dinner last night?" Victoria arched an eyebrow and nodded, putting the pieces of the food poisoning mystery into place. "So about ten hours ago. Yes. Probably ate something that wasn't quite right. A lot of vegetables, if not washed properly, can have bacteria on them. But food poisoning is no laughing matter."

"I mean, we ate completely different dishes, but I feel totally fine. I even had the prime rib, which was pretty good considering where we were. You know, they have that juice that you can dip it in and—"

"Oh my god!" Frankie cried before sticking her face in the white paper bag and retching out whatever was left in her stomach.

"She really doesn't like meat," Mara said, grabbing some paper towels from the shiny metal dispenser and handing them to Frankie before rubbing her back to comfort her.

"Clearly," Victoria agreed. She removed her stethoscope and stepped back from the table. She swapped out Frankie's paper bag for a pink, plastic, kidney-shaped bowl. A vomit dish. She looked relieved to have come through the incident unscathed. No doubt she had seen worse, but it was probably a hell of a way to start her Friday morning. "Okay. I'll send a doctor in and we'll get her started on some intravenous fluids."

Mara's mind reeled for a way to get the pretty nurse's number, trying to be slick with a puking woman in between them. "Should I ask for you if I have to bring her back in? For a follow-up or something? I don't even know your last name."

"Anyone here will be able to help you. Most likely you won't need to return. I bet Frankie will be back on her feet in no time." Victoria paused and turned back to face them before exiting the room. "I really have to say…"

Mara stood tall and proud, ready for the incoming compliment or offer to see each other again. Maybe coffee sometime. Her eyebrows raised and she bit her bottom lip in anticipation. Bring on the flirt. This one was hooked.

"Next time, take your girlfriend somewhere nicer than the five-dollar buffet."

Her *girlfriend*? Hot Nurse Victoria thought Frankie was her girlfriend?

"No, no! She's not my—" Mara stammered trying to hold Victoria's attention. She hadn't even got to the part of her spiel where she slipped in that she was in the comedy show at the Laffmoor.

But Victoria was gone, shutting the curtain behind her and missing Mara's protests all together. Frankie's muffled giggle came through her pukey paper towels.

"Oh, now you're feeling better?" Mara frowned at her friend.

"What?" Frankie squinted her red-rimmed eyes at Mara. "Serves you right for trying to pick up some chick while I'm puking my guts out."

"I was just trying to be friendly," Mara said with a casual flick of her wrist. She meant to convey a lack of interest, but she couldn't deny the weird tickle at the back of her neck. That nurse had been completely immune to her charms. It was practically an outrage. She had half a mind to follow her out into the hall and give the flirt one last try, but Frankie gave another groan and wrapped her arms around her belly. There were more pressing matters that needed her attention. Another woman needed her to get her into bed in a very different way. Mara put her arm around Frankie's shoulders. "Don't worry, we'll have you home in no time and this whole thing will be behind us."

CHAPTER FOUR

Saturday morning shifts at the hospital were always hectic, but this one really had the staff hopping. Victoria had been on her feet for hours and there didn't seem to be any end in sight. The ER was buzzing with the fallout from Friday night Vegas partying. A couple stomach pumps, several stitches, broken bones from drunken falls, and even an object lodged in a very foreign place. All typical, unfortunately.

When Victoria finally got a minute to catch her breath and grab a big, steaming mug of coffee, she sat in the nurses' station and searched for a way to appear busy while taking a quick break. Cleaning up the discarded files from past patients that had been neglected in the hustle and bustle over the last few days seemed like a good option. She took her time sorting them in alphabetical order by last name, intending to return them to the shelves in the medical records room after she was properly caffeinated.

As she sorted through the middle of the alphabet, one name jumped out at her: Malone. Frankie Malone, the food-poisoned woman and her "not girlfriend." Victoria remembered the not girlfriend's name was Mara. Victoria actually remembered a lot about her—her big, wavy, brown hair, her toned body and mostly her gorgeous, confident smile. Victoria had totally shot down Mara's hints of wanting to see her again. Picking someone up at their place of work—in the emergency room particularly—seemed too…gutsy, as if Mara was used to getting what she wanted. Like it always came easy to her. It had caught Victoria off guard, not to mention that Victoria still had mixed feelings on diving back into the dating world. She didn't need a soulmate; she didn't have time for one. She was content to be busy and focused on her career. She didn't need to be risking her heart just to go clubbing, and partying, and definitely not eating at the five-dollar buffet.

But she did need a date for her grandmother's party.

Victoria divided the files into piles for shelving and thought a little more about Mara. If she was going to dive into the dating pool for anyone, it would be a woman like that. Could Mara make her laugh? That was probably the one thing she missed most being alone—someone to share a good laugh. Well, that and of course the…

"Victoria!" Laney, one of the young nurses working the same shift, rushed up to the station. "We've got a multi-vehicle car crash coming in. All hands on deck."

The files would have to wait, along with her coffee and musing about Mara. She left the patient files on the desk and followed Laney down the hallway to the triage area by the ambulance bay. Other nurses and doctors were already assembled waiting for assignment as patients arrived. Victoria grabbed a pair of latex gloves, just as Laney intentionally bumped shoulders with her, nodding toward a tall, skinny blonde wearing a suit and holding a clipboard. "Do you know her?"

Victoria recognized the sour-pussed woman as a hospital social worker. "Do you mean Anna? Yeah. I mean, kinda. What about her?" Turning her attention back to the glass doors, she stretched up on her toes in an attempt to see if any emergency vehicles were pulling up outside.

Leave it to Laney to want to gossip about coworkers while the battered and bloodied were about to come through the door.

"I heard she's a lesbian," Laney whispered and raised her eyebrows at Victoria, as if waiting for kudos on passing on such top-shelf intel. When none came, she continued. "You should totally ask her out. Didn't you say you need a date for that party?"

Victoria eyed the social worker from across the floor. Anna's long hair was pulled into a tight knot at the nape of her neck and her mouth was puckered, as if she had been sucking lemons for the better part of the morning. Anna stopped an aide and literally wagged a finger in the young man's face while she barked orders at him. *Yeah, she seems fun.* Victoria would prefer to face the consequences of showing up at the birthday party alone than taking Anna as her date. "I don't think so."

"What do you mean, you 'don't think so?'" Laney looked incredulous as she snapped the latex against her wrist. "You haven't been on a date in forever."

"And that's just fine with me." Victoria crossed her arms defiantly. She would date again when she was good and ready. The only reason she was considering dating now was to avoid the penis parade her mother would be grand marshalling if she showed up alone to the celebration. But even that had no effect on her feelings about asking out Anna the Social Worker. "I don't want to go out with Anna. She's not my type at all."

Laney shook her head. "How can you say that? She's gay, you're gay, go for it."

She had to be freaking kidding. That reasoning was right up there with, "My cousin's girlfriend's old college roommate is gay. Do you know her?" Victoria took a deep breath before responding, summoning her most calm, even voice. "Maybe you should go out with Kevin from Ortho."

Laney's face twisted in horror at the suggestion. "Kevin with the beer gut? Nope. Not gonna happen."

"Why not?" Victoria shrugged and adopted the same tone Laney had used with her. "He's straight, you're straight, go for it."

"Ha ha, very funny." Laney narrowed her eyes, her lips formed a sarcastic grin. "It's not the same thing at all."

"Totally the same, and that concludes this debate and closes the subject indefinitely." Victoria nodded in the direction of the glass doors as paramedics began bringing in the victims of the crash. "Let's get to it."

Victoria didn't wait for Laney. She rushed into the action, much more comfortable handling an emergency situation than discussing her love life.

CHAPTER FIVE

Game of Flats had a decent crowd for a Sunday night as Penny, Frankie and Mara pushed through the women on the dark and somewhat sticky dance floor and made their way toward the bar. The place itself was a hole in the wall, but it was the only lesbian club near the strip.

Their friend Jenna was bartending, and she waved them over toward a group of empty stools at the far end. She cleared away abandoned barware and set out cardboard coasters printed with pictures of pin-up girls like she was dealing cards as they approached. "What's everybody drinking?"

Mara took the middle stool, letting her friends settle in around her. "Jack and Coke."

Penny took her seat and primly crossed her legs, fussing with the hem of her beaded tank top. "Chardonnay, please."

"Ginger ale," Frankie sighed and plopped on the last stool.

Jenna pushed at her jet-black faux-hawk with both hands and side-eyed Frankie and her drink choice. It was a definite change from Frankie's usual icy, frothy, fruity drink of choice. "What's up with that?"

"She's recovering from food poisoning," Mara said. "She puked for two days straight."

"Charming explanation," Jenna cringed.

"Well, it's the truth," Frankie replied. "I'm not taking any chances with my stomach tonight."

Jenna began pouring the drinks. "Why did you even come out? Maybe you should be resting and recovering."

"I couldn't stand being holed up in that apartment anymore. I missed you guys." Frankie smiled weakly.

After working all day Frankie probably should have stayed home and taken it easy, but it didn't surprise Mara that her usually bubbly and energetic friend had dragged herself out. Frankie was a social butterfly, and the thought of the rest of the group hanging out at Game of Flats while she sat in and watched *Gilmore Girls* reruns for another night was probably more than she could stand.

Jenna placed a tall glass of ginger ale in front of Frankie. "Just don't pass anything on to the rest of us." She wiped her hands on the bar towel hanging from her belt loop, as if to rid herself of any germs that may have made the jump from friend to friend.

"It was food poisoning," Frankie argued in a voice tinged with whininess. "It's not contagious."

"Unless she treats you to the five-dollar buffet," Mara quipped. "The real question is what's the deal with the crowd in here tonight?"

There was no doubt Game of Flats was busier than usual for a Sunday. Every seat at the bar was taken and the dance floor was thumping and full of patrons. Even most of the tables lining the far wall were full. Something was different.

"It's the new DJ," Jenna said. "She's quite a hit with the ladies."

As Jenna moved to take care of her customers, Mara sat up straighter on her stool to get a better look at the woman in the DJ booth. She wanted to see this girl who was making such an impression on the Flats crowd. The DJ was young, probably early twenties, with tanned skin and long, dark hair pulled into a ponytail under her headphones. Her style was very Sporty Spice in a black tank top and rainbow striped wristbands. "I can see why she's such a hit. She's hot," Mara observed.

"You think everyone is hot." Penny rolled her eyes at her best friend, but then peered back over own her shoulder to get a glimpse of the DJ anyway.

"I do not!" Mara protested between sips, although she did consider herself open to the many types and styles of women out there. "She's a good-looking woman. I was merely agreeing with the general consensus."

"You so do," Frankie agreed and gave Mara a pursed-lipped, get real look. "You're a player. Heck, you even hit on that nurse while I was dying the other night."

"That went nowhere fast." Mara smirked, not thrilled to rehash her flirt fail from the emergency room. "Thanks, by the way, for the clitorference."

"Whatever, dude. Like you're hurting for a date. Play on, playa." Frankie winked.

Penny's well-sculpted eyebrows arched up with interest as she turned back to face Mara. "What nurse the other night? Why didn't I hear about this nurse?"

"Because there was nothing to tell." Mara shrugged feigning indifference in an attempt to shut the subject down.

But Frankie went on anyway, oblivious to Mara's signals. "Yeah, she went all googly-eyed over the nurse who checked me out while I was vomiting up a lung."

Disgust crossed Penny's face. "You two need to knock it off with your regurgitation talk. It's gross. Let's move on."

"Fine." Mara seized the opportunity to redirect the discussion back to the DJ. "But Penny, you can't deny you think that chick is above average in hotness."

"She's attractive but too young for my taste. Besides, I have a woman. I don't need to be scoping out DJ or anyone else for that matter." Just talking about Lauren seemed to make Penny relax again.

"Ah, scoping out the DJ, eh?" Jenna nodded knowingly as she returned to their end of the bar and gestured at the dance floor in front of the booth. "Look at those poor saps clamoring for her, and she's so into her music, she doesn't even seem to notice. Or maybe she really just doesn't care. Who knows?"

Penny pushed her glass across the surface of the bar toward Jenna. "No, we are not scoping out the DJ. I'm going to need another one of these."

"Is Hayleigh working tonight?" Mara asked as Jenna poured the Chardonnay.

"Yep. Dancing on the bar over at Howler's."

"Oh! Game of Flats should hire bar dancers." Frankie's face lit up making her look almost like her normal self. "Then you and Hayleigh could work together!"

"Hell no," Jenna retorted. "Have every lesbian in town fawning over my girl like they do the DJ? No fucking way."

Jenna and Hayleigh had U-Hauled to Las Vegas from a small town in Oklahoma a year and a half earlier. Mara was dating Frankie at the time and they all met when Jenna and Hayleigh adopted Rex, a German shepherd/black lab mix, from the animal shelter. Frankie made friends with them easily, as she always did with people, and they started hanging around Café Gato. Hayleigh was chasing her dream of being a showgirl while biding her time with gigs like magician's assistant, nightclub hostess, and her latest job, scantily-clad bar-top dancer.

"Just a suggestion." Frankie shrugged then shifted on her barstool. "Mara, don't forget the meeting for everyone involved in the shelter fundraiser tomorrow morning. Nine o'clock sharp. Is it on your calendar?"

Mara groaned. Monday morning meetings were not a regular occurrence for her, and even though she was happy to help Frankie out, she regretted agreeing to any event that close to daybreak. "Nine o'clock on a Monday morning? Why does it have to be so early? And what makes you think I own a calendar?"

"You promised." Frankie pouted. "So be there. Or be… square."

"Lord help me, I sure don't want to be square! Instead I'll attend a nine a.m. meeting. Nothing square about that." Mara drained her glass. She sucked an ice cube and attempted to ignore Frankie's hard, expectant stare. Mara's indifference didn't last long. It never did when it came to her friends. "Okay, okay. I'll be there."

CHAPTER SIX

As Mara expected, nine o'clock Monday morning felt like a brick to the head. It was her own fault for hanging around in the casino after leaving Game of Flats but knowing that didn't make her alarm clock buzzing any kinder when it went off at seven thirty. She made it to Café Gato just in the nick of time for the meeting, and she was pushing her sunglasses onto the top of her head when Frankie rushed over to greet her.

"Yay! You made it!"

She wrapped her arms around Mara in a bigger hug than her appearance at the meeting warranted. She was obviously back to good health and operating at full, enthusiastic power. When she finally let go of the embrace but continued standing in front of Mara, blocking her path to the chairs set up for the meeting, it was clear something was up.

"What's going on? What is…" Mara circled a finger pointing out the lack of space between the two women. "This?"

"Nothing!" Frankie's overly-happy expression remained for just a moment longer before she dropped it entirely with a shoulder sagging sigh. "Okay. I have something to tell you, but it's not a big deal. I don't want you to panic or freak out or anything. We don't need any weird vibes here at this meeting today. Maybe we should go get you some coffee first." She took Mara's arm to steer her toward the coffee bar. Mara wiggled her shoulders, attempting to shrug out of her grasp.

"Frankie, just tell me what the hell it is." As Mara raised up on her toes, weaving and bobbing back and forth to see past her friend's body block, she caught a glimpse of the dozen or so people already assembled in the rows of chairs Frankie had set up for her presentation. One woman in particular stood out—the ER nurse.

She sat up straight in her chair, a jewel-toned paisley scarf trailing over her slender back, along with her long red hair. Hair that had caught Mara's attention the first time they had met in the emergency room. The nurse who shot her down. Heat flushed Mara's core and moved its way up to her neck. She was equally drawn to the attractive woman and embarrassed from her failed attempt to get her phone number at the hospital. It was a foreign sensation to Mara. Her stomach twisted along with the conflicting emotions. "What the hell is she doing here?"

"Yeah, I know. Listen." Frankie put a comforting hand on Mara's shoulder to draw her attention back from the ER nurse. "She's only sitting in for the publicity rep from Emerald Isle today. It's not like she's going to be involved with the whole project. Get over yourself, suck up your pride, and just get through this meeting. Do it for me because you promised. Her being here is not a big deal. There's an open seat by Bob. Go sit by him and we'll get started."

"Bob? Ugh." Mara disappointedly eyed up the balding public relations coordinator from the Rothmoor. She should have known he would be the one attending the meeting in Penny's place. "I don't want to sit by Bob. He's no fun."

"This isn't supposed to be fun." Frankie pursed her lips and moved her hands to her hips in a no-nonsense stance. "This is business. And it's very important to me. So please. Just sit."

Mara clamped her jaw tightly shut to keep herself from saying any more. Frankie was right. She needed to focus on the matter at hand and not worry about sitting next to some boring dude and not getting distracted by some pretty face who had given her the cold shoulder. Nodding but silent, she turned her mouth up into what she hoped came across as a confident smile and took the chair next to Bob.

"Good morning," Mara greeted him as she got comfortable in her seat.

He returned her smile, but his dark beady eyes were tinged with red and more watery than usual. All the good graces Mara had just promised Frankie she would uphold melted away at the sight of him. "What the hell happened to you?"

His shoulders slumped in his short-sleeve, size-too-big button up shirt. "I'm allergic to cats." He couldn't have sounded more pathetic. "As soon as I walked in, three of them came right up to me and started circling my legs. They were like sharks surrounding a bloody carcass in the water. I swear they saw me coming. It's like they knew. They want to cause me misery. It's their mission."

"I'm sure they just thought you looked like a nice man who would give them attention." Even cats recognized Bob as easy prey. Poor guy.

Fortunately before Mara had to hear any more about sad sack Bob's miserable morning, Frankie called the meeting to order. She launched into her speech about the needs of the animal shelter and how businesses helping the shelter are building up the community, blah, blah, blah.

Mara was behind Frankie one hundred percent in this endeavor already. She didn't need convincing. She fixed that pleasant smile back on her face and let her mind wander.

Of course, it wandered right down the opposite end of the row from where she was sitting, directly to the fiery-haired nurse and her fiery spirit to match. At least that was how it came across when she turned Mara down. Mara liked feisty women. She was much more attracted to ambitious, driven women who went after what they wanted. That often meant they were a tougher nut to crack. And Mara hadn't exactly been her charming best after sitting in the waiting room all that time with Frankie. Maybe it was just a case of getting off on the wrong foot. One failure wouldn't hold her back. In fact, the more she thought about it, the more it seemed like their meeting in the ER was just not the best place for her to make her move. It hardly seemed like an actual failure at all. It was more like an opportunity to get a foot in the door. It was just a first attempt and she wouldn't mind the chance to make a second impression on the pretty nurse. A much better, notable impression.

Mara glanced down the row to where the woman was studiously scribbling notes on a yellow legal pad. Smart and efficient, the nurse-turned-casino rep kept getting better and better. Victoria was dressed in neat khaki capris and chunky wedge espadrilles with pink ribbon wraps around her slim ankles. Business casual and sexy all rolled into one. Yeah, Mara wanted that second chance for sure. Her eyes travelled up Victoria's body to her face. Her lips formed a heart while she focused on the presentation going on in front of them. Mara considered what it would be like to kiss those lips, slide her tongue across them. Her nipples went hard at the thought.

As if she felt the heat of Mara's stare, Victoria's long-lashed eyes flicked down the row of seats. Busted. Mara smiled and did a little inconspicuous wave. *She doesn't know what you were thinking… She doesn't know what you were thinking. Be cool.*

Victoria's expression softened with recognition and the corners of her mouth turned up as she gave a slight, shy, friendly nod.

Mara's cheeks went hot like a blush. Except she didn't blush. Ever. It was probably just getting warm in the café with all the people seated on one side of it. The temperature in the café probably just shifted from cool to hot. Mara quickly looked away from Victoria, breaking eye contact. That was enough of a reunion for the moment. Mara's thoughts were interrupted by a thin, gray cat who had snuck between the seats and suddenly leapt onto Bob's lap.

Bob promptly sneezed.

"Geez, Bob. I had no idea you attracted so much pussy."

Mara knocked her shoulder into her coworker's pathetically slumped form beside her, pretty damn pleased with her own joke. At least she was pleased until she realized Frankie had stopped talking and the titter of stifled laughter around her indicated that her words had been heard by more people than just Bob, including sexy Nurse Victoria, who had a palm pressed against her beautiful heart-shaped lips as if she had stopped a potential spit take involving the coffee she had been sipping.

So much for that better second impression.

"As I was saying…" Frankie tried to recapture the attention of the group, her hard stare on Mara, expressing her displeasure at the ill-timing of the joke. "That's all I have for you today. Please email me with the details of your business's donations. If you are interested in helping out with preparations for the event, I have a sign-up sheet on this table. The more volunteers we get, the smoother the night will run. And the more successful the night is, the better the publicity will be for all parties involved. So don't be shy. Thanks again for coming out this morning. If anyone wants to go over and see the animal shelter, I would be happy to give you a tour."

The squeaking of chairs sliding against the linoleum floor and the shuffling of feet and paper as people collected their belongings filled the café. Mara turned and put her hand on Bob's shoulder. "No tours of the animal shelter for you, okay? I'll sign up to volunteer to help. Go take a Claritin or something."

Bob gave a watery-eyed, half-smile before making a beeline for the exit, leaving Mara standing alone among the publicity reps who all seemed to know each other. It seemed like a good time to apologize to Frankie for interrupting her presentation.

Mara cautiously approached her friend at the sign up table. "Hey. Sorry about that pussy thing."

"Right. You just can't help yourself. I know," Frankie muttered. She fussed with the placement of the pen on the table a moment longer before whispering sternly, "I am trying to conduct a serious business thingy and you're cracking P jokes.

Thanks for the support." Sweet Frankie couldn't even bring herself to say the word *pussy*.

Mara slid her arms around Frankie's waist and tipped her head onto her shoulder. "I am sorry, Frankie. And you know I am one hundred percent in on this event—whatever you want me to do."

"Good." Frankie's voice regained its usual bubbly tone as she rifled through the stack of papers in front of her, pulling out a single sheet and holding it out. "What I want you to do is head up the decorations for the night. Look, you already have a volunteer to help you."

Mara eyed the sheet and the only name written on it in a happy, flowery script: Victoria McHenry. Her second, actually third chance. Snapping her head up, Mara looked over to where the nurse had been sitting. Victoria's chair had been abandoned, but Mara spotted her heading to the bin to return her coffee mug. "Be right back."

She rushed over to Nurse Victoria. "Hi. Um, remember me?" Mara tapped her on the shoulder, startling her, but Victoria was smiling when she turned around. "Mara. We met at—"

"The hospital. I remember." She nodded. "I'm glad to see Frankie made a full recovery."

"Yeah, she's resilient like that. So, uh, I seem to be in charge of the decorations for the party." Mara waved the paper she held in her hand in the air like that proved something. "And you seem to be my only volunteer. So, I thought maybe we could get together and knock some ideas around. Are you up for that?"

Victoria raised her eyebrows, looking a little taken aback by the suggestion, but she recovered quickly. "Oh, sure. I just…I'm just standing in for my sister today. She's actually the point of contact for the Emerald Isle. I put my name and number down instead of hers because she might be a little hard to reach right now. She's in the mountains. Skiing." She paused and drew in her breath.

It was an overexplanation. An excuse. Too much. She was trying to bow out gracefully. That had to be it. Mara sucked up her disappointment and said, "Then I should contact your sister instead? That's okay. If you want to give me her number, I can call her after she's back in town."

"No," Victoria said quickly, boosting her tan, buttery leather tote on her shoulder. "I mean, you'll probably need to start planning as soon as possible since the event is only three weeks away. I could meet with you before Maddie gets back and then hand everything off to her when she returns."

Mara's lip twitched. A goofy grin attempted to spread across her face. *Don't be a dork.* Why was talking to Victoria making her nervous? Women didn't make her nervous. "Are you free for coffee tomorrow?"

Victoria bit her lip and shook her head. "I work the day shift for the rest of the week. How about we meet for a drink around seven?"

"Perfect. At Game of Flats? Do you know where that is? We'll just be casual, bounce some ideas off each other." Game of Flats was like home court advantage. They could start out planning, take care of what they needed to get back to Frankie, and then Mara could make her move on Victoria.

"Sounds good. I've got to run but you have my number if anything comes up." Victoria gave her a coy smile. "You can call or text, whatever."

Mara pressed her lips together and nodded solemnly, trying to stay cool in spite of her inward excitement at the idea of a real chance to finally make a good impression on her. "I'll do that. And thanks."

"For what?" Victoria tipped her head to the side regarding Mara curiously, a cute, innocent look that gave Mara a flutter in her stomach.

Mara turned on that million-dollar smile that always won women over. "For offering to help. I wouldn't want to go it all alone."

"You bet." Victoria gave her a nod, her eyelashes fluttering over bright green eyes, before she headed out of the café.

Mara was still watching Victoria push through the front door and disappear out into the blinding Vegas sun when Frankie came up behind her. "That seemed to go much better than last time," Frankie said, squeezing Mara's shoulder, a gesture showing she was over the ill-timed joke from earlier.

"Indeed, it did." Mara couldn't hold back her grin any longer.

"Just don't blow it tomorrow, playa."

Mara smiled confidently. She was too excited about the prospect of seeing Victoria again to let her friend get to her. "Don't worry. I've got this."

CHAPTER SEVEN

Victoria went straight home from Café Gato, wanting a little down time before grocery shopping and the other errands she did on her day off. Her mind was stuck on Mara and their upcoming meeting for drinks. She hadn't been all that quick to act on her sister's behalf, but if it meant getting to spend a little more time with Mara, it might just be worth it. Victoria may as well get something out of the whole "covering for Maddie" thing, and that something could very well be a date for her grandmother's birthday party. It wasn't her worst idea. Stranger things had happened.

Mara's joke during the meeting had cracked Victoria up so much that coffee almost came out of her nose. The inappropriate timing had made it all the more humorous. It was the best laugh she'd had in a long while, and that made her think that maybe Mara was someone she would like to get to know better. *Definitely*.

Buddy greeted her as soon as she walked into the house. He purred and repeatedly wove his gray body between her legs until she scooped him up and kissed the soft fur on the top of his little kitty head.

"Hey there, precious boy," she murmured into his fur. "I've met someone. Someone interesting."

Oh, she had actually said it out loud. Someone interesting. It was weird to admit, even to herself. It had been so long since she had acknowledged any feelings like that—finding someone interesting in that way—but this woman had set something off in her. It was like she'd been sleepwalking through life and was now shaking off the dream world, ready to bask in the morning sun.

No. This was not that. This was just her needing a date for the party. That was all.

Probably.

Buddy meowed but Victoria suspected it could be because she was holding him too tightly and not an actual response to her revelation. He wriggled and she put him back down, where he quickly scampered off to his water dish. Not exactly the conversation she was craving.

She fished her keys out of her pocket and hung them on one of the little hooks by the door, catching her reflection in the mirror above it. She grinned. "She's interesting and quite good looking." Although pleased with her happy expression, there was not a conversation to be had there either.

It was a desperate move, but she did the only thing she could think of to have someone to actually talk to—she picked up her cell and called Maddie. She was stunned when her sister actually answered.

"Hi, Vicki. How was the meeting? Did you take notes?"

Victoria ignored the second question, knowing damn well that had Maddie attended the meeting herself, she would have spent the entire time chit-chatting with the people around her and not writing down one word about the actual event. "It went fine. The Café Gato is very cute. The fundraiser seems like a great one for Emerald Isle to be involved with. And I met a woman there and I think it could be something."

"Something, like, good for business?" Maddie sounded distracted or possibly disinterested.

"No. Good for me." Victoria blew out a big breath. Was she really going to admit this to her sister, knowing what a can of worms she would be opening? But she had to talk to someone about it. She really needed to make some friends. "I'm… interested in her. We made plans to meet up."

Maddie let out a whoop on the other end of the line. Victoria could only imagine how relieved her sister was that she was expanding her social life. "That's awesome! See? I told you getting out in the community would be good for you."

"I mean, I might be," Victoria backtracked. It wasn't a date or anything like that, but it sure felt as if Mara had been flirting with her. She hoped Mara had been flirting with her, unless she had read it all wrong. Maybe the whole thing was nothing more than a meeting to accomplish the goal of the decorating committee for the fundraiser just as stated? Maybe she had imagined the chemistry between her and Mara.

"So who is this mystery woman?" Maddie pressed.

Victoria sighed. The shadow of doubt that had crept into her brain made her regret calling Maddie. "It's the woman you'll be working with when you get back and take this project over. Her name is Mara Antonini. We're meeting for drinks and discussing ideas for decorations. I guess it's not really that big of a deal."

"Mara Antonini? The comedian from the Rothmoor?" Maddie had snapped back to full attention. "You're interested in Mara Antonini and you're going out with her for drinks?"

"Yep. Mara Antonini," Victoria confirmed. She hitched her hip onto the arm of the couch to perch. "And if things go well, she could end up being my date for Grandmother's birthday party."

Maddie laughed a rolling, haughty laugh. "Oh, no, no, no. Mara Antonini isn't the girl you want to set your sights on for your party date. She's not that kind of girl."

"What the hell is that supposed to mean?"

"Victoria, don't get all mad at me about it." The eye roll in Maddie's tone was perfectly clear. "Everyone in town knows Mara Antonini. She's a total playgirl, definitely not the kind you're going to pin down and mold into the perfect girlfriend."

"Total playgirl? How would you even know that?"

"Julia Matson told me. She hooked up with Mara one night and then never heard from her again. Mara totally ghosted her." Maddie presented her evidence with complete smugness. "And Julia isn't even gay!"

"Well, it sounds like she was that night," Victoria observed as she shifted on the couch arm. But Maddie had planted her seed of doubt. It figured. The one person who had actually caught Victoria's interest had a "love 'em and leave 'em" reputation. Her heart sunk. She wasn't down for trying to convert an established playgirl into the quintessential prom date like some kind of '90s teen movie. She needed something she could work with, not an outrageous long shot who was looking to score.

At least she had found out about Mara before she had become too invested or done anything she would regret. Any hopes of dating Mara so they could become a couple in time for the birthday party was evaporating like a puddle in the Vegas sun. The only reason Victoria had even considered wanting to ask Mara to be her date was because Maddie and Laney had been harassing her about her love life anyway. She should just let the subject drop and turn off those feelings. Meet Mara for drinks, talk decorations, and keep it strictly business.

"I'm just passing on information," Maddie said. "Don't shoot the messenger and all that."

"You know what? I'm not really that into her. It's just a meeting about decorations, and I'll get the details to you right after I get home from it." Victoria completely regretted her decision to confide in her sister. She needed a way to take it all back. Her mind raced for a distraction, when she heard a deep voice in the background on the other end of the line, followed by the sound of activity. The activity sounded suspiciously like two people snuggling together—ruffling sheets, low grunts of voices. "Is everything okay there?"

"Oh, yeah. I'm just… Well, Gregory just walked in and he wants to grab something to eat."

"Gregory?" A new name as far as Victoria was concerned. Apparently Maddie was expanding her social circle as well. He presented the perfect distraction from Victoria's situation.

"Uh-huh. We met last night," Maddie whispered. "He's a self-made millionaire and hot as fuck, so…we're going to have brunch. I've gotta run but good luck with the comedian." She clicked off the call without waiting for Victoria to say anything more. Typical Maddie behavior—a hot, rich guy comes around and everything else just drops away.

At least Victoria had been spared any further discussion about her feelings for Mara. Now all she had to do was figure out how to make them go away.

CHAPTER EIGHT

"Frankie tells me you're meeting that nurse from the ER for drinks," Penny said, wiggling her eyebrows while simultaneously stabbing her fork at the chopped veggies in her salad. A true talent.

"Wow, news travels fast around here." Mara laughed in an attempt to make her tone as easy-breezy, casual as possible. "It's not a date or anything. We're working on decorations for the animal shelter fundraiser."

Mara shoved a forkful of pasta in her mouth, hoping that would be the end of the discussion. Full mouth, no talking. It was bad enough she had repeatedly acted like a bumbling idiot in front of Victoria. She didn't need the whole world to know about her trials. The only thing she had scheduled with the woman was a get together to work on the decorations. No sense in letting her friends get the wrong idea.

That was the thing about their circle of friends. Once one person knew something, they all did. It had its plusses, like when everyone rallied around Hayleigh after a bad audition, but sometimes it wasn't so great, like the meeting with Victoria blowing up from something that was not a big deal to huge, exciting, juicy proportions. It really wasn't a date. Mara didn't date. Besides, Victoria had probably only agreed to the get together to help her sister out. That was it. Victoria hadn't been the least bit shy about shooting Mara down the day they met in the hospital. The more Mara thought about it, the more her hopefulness from the day before waned. No, it wasn't a date.

"So who is this woman anyway?" Penny pressed. "All Frankie told me was that she was the nurse that took care of her in the emergency room last week. Tell me more about her."

"Of course Frankie did," Mara muttered, wiping marinara from her mouth with a napkin to buy a little time before answering. "She's just sitting in for her sister who's the publicity rep for the Emerald Isle Casino. I probably won't even see her again after tomorrow. It's just a meeting to talk about the fundraiser."

"Wait a minute." Penny's fork clanked against her plate as she dropped her hand, stopping all other action to focus on Mara. "Did you say Emerald Isle?"

"Yeah. Emerald Isle."

"You're talking about Vicki McHenry, right? That's who you have a drinks date with? You've got the hots for Vicki?" Penny gave her a sour look. It was more than her "missing Lauren" cranky look. She was clearly not pleased with the turn the conversation had taken.

"Well," Mara began cautiously, "like I mentioned, it's not a date. And I don't have the…It's not a date. Her name is Victoria."

"Vicki McHenry, right?"

"Victoria," Mara repeated. "Yeah, McHenry. Her sister works for Emerald Isle."

"Her father *owns* Emerald Isle."

It was Mara's turn to do the jaw-drop thing. Victoria's father owned the Emerald Isle Casino? She shook her head in disbelief. "Are you sure?"

"Yes, I'm sure. I've known the McHenry family forever. Vicki and I went to high school together." Penny set her utensils on her plate in the five o'clock position and wiped her hands on the napkin.

Mara sighed hard and stabbed at her pasta. She hadn't expected this bump in the road. "What's the problem?"

"Nothing." Penny crossed her arms, but her walls up mode didn't last long under Mara's persistent stare. "Fine. There's a past there, but it was high school. It's…whatever."

Mara raised her brows at her best friend, knowing Penny way too well to buy her "whatever," but it didn't seem like Penny was going to disclose anything further.

Great. The one woman who had really caught Mara's eye lately ended up being her best friend's "whatever." Mara didn't want to stop pursuing Victoria. She was way too intrigued by the beautiful redhead, and the chase was delicious. But Penny was Mara's best friend, and she didn't want to cause her discomfort or…*whatever*. It was better that she found out now that Victoria and Penny had a past before anything happened between them.

That was that. Mara would meet with Victoria, take care of business, and then let it go. It would be okay. Easy come, easy go. Victoria didn't seem especially interested in her that night in the emergency room anyway. No need to push it. There were thousands of women in Vegas. This one just wasn't meant to be. She would just meet Victoria, talk decorations, and they would go their separate ways.

Victoria wasn't the girl for her. No big deal. Plenty of fish in the sea. All the comforting clichés ran through Mara's mind, but there was a burning in the pit of her stomach that she suspected had nothing to do with the lunch she just ate. If Victoria McHenry didn't matter that much to her, then why did she feel like she'd lost something?

CHAPTER NINE

Game of Flats was busier than Mara expected on a Tuesday night. The new DJ was obviously still working her magic, keeping the music pumping and the ladies begging for more.

While Jenna poured her a Jack and Coke, Mara kept her eye on the door. She had been repeating the plan in her mind all evening: say hello, get down to business, schedule a time to meet Victoria's sister, and get the hell out. All Mara had to do was get through this one little meeting with Victoria and she wouldn't have to see her again.

"Is Hayleigh working tonight?" Mara took a tentative sip from her glass, trying to distract herself from her thoughts of Victoria.

"No." Jenna grimaced. "She'll be in later. Stick around after your meeting. I'm sure she'd like the company until I'm off."

With Hayleigh working her new bar dancing job until all hours of the night, and Mara being tied up with the afternoon show at the Laffmoor every day, the friends hadn't seen much of each other lately. It would be good to catch up, and it would give her another excuse to cut the meeting with Victoria short. Mara nodded in agreement. "Sounds good."

"Why are you staring at the door like that? Are you nervous about meeting with this chick?" Jenna eyed her suspiciously. "You *are* nervous. What do you have to be squeamish about? Are you into her?"

"What?" Mara twisted on the barstool, faced Jenna and took another gulp of her drink to further exude nonchalance. She certainly didn't have to rehash her weird conversation with Penny earlier. "No, I'm not nervous and no, I'm not into her. I just want to get this over with."

"Well, good luck with that. It's show time." Jenna nodded in the direction of the door before moving down the bar to take someone else's order.

Mara glanced up to see Victoria coming in, looking hotter than ever in tight jeans, high strappy heels and a silky, light blue tank top. She downed the rest of her drink and waved to get the pretty woman's attention.

As Victoria sauntered over, Mara slid off the barstool chanting her mantra for the evening in her head: strictly business, strictly business… "Hello!"

"Hi!" Victoria surprised Mara with a hug.

Pressed against Victoria she caught a whiff of citrusy perfume. The effect was slightly dizzying. Her "strictly business" plan was going to be a lot harder to execute than she had originally thought.

"Should we grab a booth?" Victoria continued. If Mara's expression had given away the fuzzy-headed bubbly feeling she had experienced during their embrace, Victoria had missed it. "Somewhere we can talk? It's really loud in here."

Mara nodded and pointed to an empty table against the wall. When they had both slid into the curved seat she said in a loud voice over the music, "It's the new DJ. She's so popular, I guess they've brought her in more nights. I wasn't thinking when I suggested this place."

"We could just go to my place instead. It's not far," Victoria suggested.

The way Victoria presented it sounded innocent enough. They were only going to Victoria's place because it was impossible to hear anything in the bar. It was just to take care of the business at hand. Mara could go over, they would do what they needed to do, and she could get the hell out of there. Mara could even make it back to Flats to meet Hayleigh afterward. Most of all, Penny would never know, and it wouldn't matter anyway, because that would be the end of it. Mara would not be distracted by the plunging neckline of Victoria's top or the way the pink gloss shimmered on her lips.

"I have wine." Victoria upped the ante at Mara's hesitation.

"In that case, I'm in." Mara grinned with a wink and then immediately regretted it. A wink was not business-like at all. Must. Stick. To. The. Plan.

The ten-minute cab ride provided just enough time for the women to decide on a fifties-style sock hop with an animal spin as the theme for the fundraiser at Café Gato. They called it "Bark Around The Clock." There would be a soda fountain and a dance floor with a jukebox playing golden oldies from the era to set the mood. They would pull out all the stops and have a whole set built to transform the café for the event. Victoria suggested a penny candy station and a malt shop counter. Mara thought a photo booth with props like poodle skirts, Davey Crockett style hats, and 3D glasses would be fun.

Mara offered to run the plan past Frankie, get her to sign off on the theme, and to recruit additional volunteers for their committee. Victoria said her sister would go online to order the decorations and hire someone to build the set needed to bring the idea to life. Everything was divided up easy-peasy. They clearly made a good team.

Mara was struck by the slightest pang of disappointment. She would be working with Victoria's sister Maddie going forward, not Victoria. It was a shame since they had clicked so well, their creativity meshing, each one feeding off the other's ideas. Still, probably for the best considering the Penny factor. Mara wasn't supposed to be feeling hopeful feelings about Victoria. Friends before flings and all that.

"Well, that was easy. We work well together," Mara said. The words were out of her mouth before she could stop them and her cheeks went warm. Blushing again? What the hell? Mara didn't blush over women. Or anything. Especially not the woman she promised her best friend she would steer clear of. "We didn't even need the wine."

"True, but would you like to come in for a glass anyway? My house is just up ahead."

The setting sun provided Mara just enough light to get a decent look at the bungalow-style homes that lined the street. A cute, quiet little neighborhood that somehow seemed to suit Victoria. Mara could picture her fitting right in with the picket fences, manicured patches of lawn and porch swings. Victoria gardened in her spare time from the look of the colorful bursts of flowers among the landscaping that came in to view as they pulled up to her house.

Mara liked it—the cute little houses, the sunny flowers, the friendly front porches. Living in the casino had made her miss that kind of homey stuff. She wanted to know more about this woman who lived in a bungalow. Penny had said they had a past. She hadn't said anything about Mara and Victoria not being able to be friends. Just because Penny wasn't a Victoria fan didn't mean Mara had to go all *Mean Girls* on her. One drink certainly wouldn't hurt anything.

Mara smiled and dug through her wallet for cab fare. "I'd like that."

Victoria placed a hand over hers, stilling Mara with her touch. "I've got this. I was coming here anyway."

The inside of Victoria's house wasn't what Mara had expected at all—plush, comfy sofa and armchair in the living room—all neutrals, except for the bright colored throws on them, and a big screen TV mounted on the wall. This was clearly the home of a woman who enjoyed a cozy night in, further evidenced by the multiple racks of DVDs lined up against the wall. While Victoria went to pour the wine, Mara investigated the titles.

"Is Pinot noir okay?" Victoria called from the kitchen.

"Perfect." Mara scanned the racks of movies all arranged in alphabetical order, finding several of her favorite titles among them. *Airplane*, *Caddyshack*, *Home Alone*—old school comedy classics. "You have all seven *Police Academy* movies?"

Victoria handed her a glass. "What would a DVD collection be without them?"

"I love so many of these films." Mara smiled as she continued to scan the titles. "I watched a ton of this stuff when I was a kid. It just fit my sense of humor. I was always cracking jokes, even back then. My mom used to say it was because I was the baby of the family and always trying to get attention. I mean, it worked."

"It must still be working for you." Victoria studied her face. "I hear you rock the afternoon show at the Laffmoor."

Mara's cheeks went hot again. Why did that keep happening? "Thanks. I try." She turned her gaze back to the DVDs, hoping her blush would fade quickly. More importantly, hoping Victoria didn't see it.

"Did you want to put it in?"

"What?" Mara's attention snapped right back to Victoria's shining green eyes.

"*Police Academy*." Victoria tipped her head in the direction of the DVD rack. "Wanna watch?"

Oh, right. The movie. Of course. Staying for a movie was longer than only staying for a drink, but what the hell? Friends had wine and watched movies together all the time. Mara and Victoria could be friends. There was nothing wrong with that. *Nothing*. "Sure."

An hour later, the women were curled up on the couch, two glasses of wine in, thoroughly entertained by *Police Academy*. And when they both said, "Don't move, dirtbag!" along with Cadet Laverne Hooks on the screen, their giggles turned into belly laughs that lasted until they had tears streaming down their faces.

"I say it every time," Mara confessed.

Victoria swiped at the dampness on her face. "Me too." She reached over and covered Mara's hand with hers.

A tingle ran up Mara's arm and reverberated in her chest. The touch was more than friendly, that was obvious. Damn it. She didn't feel the slightest urge to pull away either, despite her best friend's past with Victoria. Instead she enjoyed Victoria's silky soft skin against hers. She wanted more contact. Mara's brown eyes locked on Victoria's green ones, and she licked her lips, hinting at her true desire.

There's a past. Penny's words echoed somewhere in the far corners of Mara's mind, but the butterflies that erupted in her belly as Victoria ran her fingertips up her thigh, presented a strong argument to press on. So the beautiful woman sitting beside her with the light sprinkling of freckles across the bridge of her nose, sparkling eyes, and bewitching smile had a past. Who didn't?

Mara's lips were suddenly so close to Victoria's. The other woman's breath was warm on her cheek. There must be some sort of statute of limitations on high school feelings. Surely Penny would forgive her this one transgression.

Victoria's eyes fluttered shut as she leaned in to kiss Mara, softly at first, then with a growing urgency. Mara relaxed into her, wrapping her arms around Victoria's slim waist and pulling her close. Victoria's tongue slipped between Mara's lips just enough to tease her, tempt her. It was the kind of kiss that left a woman craving more.

More was exactly what Mara couldn't have, or at least what she wasn't supposed to have if she was respecting Penny's past. *Fuck.* The logic in her brain wrestled with absolutely every other impulse in her body until finally Mara broke the kiss. She jolted back on the sofa away from Victoria and struggled to catch her breath, slow her quick-beating heart, and stop her racing mind. She wanted nothing more than to rush Victoria into the bedroom and have a night of crazy, delicious sex. But Penny was Mara's best friend and she couldn't just ignore that weird vibe that surrounded their discussion of Victoria McHenry. She had to get out of the house fast, before things snowballed, before there was no turning back.

"I...I have to go," Mara stammered a pathetic excuse that clearly wasn't making any sense to Victoria, whose expression was a mask of confusion and possibly…hurt? "I, uh, didn't think I'd be this late and I have to go."

Victoria's eyebrows scrunched together and her hands clenched into fists. Her previously relaxed posture was gone and she sat up stick straight as if she was on high alert. "Is something wrong? Can I get you something?"

"No, I'm fine." Mara stood and glanced around the living room. Was there something she was forgetting? The front door. Just go to the front door and walk out.

"Let me at least call you a cab," Victoria offered, but she still hadn't moved from her spot on the couch. It was a strictly autopilot response.

Mara bolted toward the door, pulling her phone out as she grabbed the doorknob. "I'll just call an Uber. Really, I'll be fine. Thanks for everything. I'll be in touch about the decorations."

She flew into the cool night air without waiting for a response from Victoria. It was no doubt the least-smooth exit she had ever made from a woman's place. As she poked at her phone to order her ride, she couldn't shake the hurt look on Victoria's face.

Mara may have spared Penny's feelings, but she had a suspicion she had screwed something else up. Big time.

CHAPTER TEN

"You kissed her?" Frankie's question voice had the habit of sliding upward at the end. Sometimes her regular sentences did too. Frankie had grown up in Southern California, so Mara attributed it to her having a bona fide valley girl as a mother. The Valley ran deep in that one. "Even though Penny has some kind of weird past with her?"

Mara had gone straight to Café Gato after leaving Victoria's house, in the hopes she would catch Frankie before she left for the night. She needed someone to talk this through with, and even though Jenna and Hayleigh were still at Game of Flats, this was more of a talk-to-Frankie situation. Now facing her friend's reaction to the events of the evening, she wondered if she should have gone back for a couple shots with the girls or just called it a night and retreated to her apartment.

"Any chance you know what that weird past is?"

"No. Sorry. But if she reacted that way there must be some story there." Frankie had taken a minute to sit down with Mara after bringing her a cup of decaf coffee and a brown sugar crumb cake muffin. "Of course you just couldn't help yourself, playa. You had to kiss her anyway. You are never going to change, are you?"

Mara set her mug down on the table a little harder than necessary and coffee sloshed over the rim. "Why the hell do you keep saying that? Do you have some grievance to air that I don't know about? Did I do you wrong when we dated?"

"Oh, no, honey. Not at all." Frankie grabbed a napkin and cleaned up the spill, not missing a beat. "It's just ever since we broke up, you haven't had a solid go at a relationship. Not even one. You just jump from chick to chick. Fling City. Like, seriously, are you ever going to settle down?"

"What can I say? I hump, I jump. Rinse and repeat." Mara rolled her eyes. "You've ruined me for other women."

"I'm serious." Frankie gave Mara's arm a quick squeeze as if to soften the blow of her harsh tone.

"I can have a relationship," Mara argued. "I like Kat just fine."

Frankie shook her head. "No, that doesn't count. She's someone you're attracted to and have fun with, and it's actually perfect for you because she leaves and you don't ever have to deal with real relationship stuff. That's not the same thing at all." Frankie paused and then said, "Wait, wasn't she supposed to come into town this week?"

"She was. Her trip got postponed a couple of weeks."

"Anyway, no, that's not the same thing at all." Frankie raised her eyebrows at Mara, daring her to argue the point further.

It was true that Mara was a total "work before love" person. Establishing her career took all of her time, which made the whole thing with Kat work for her. And if the feelings that had stirred up from kissing Victoria didn't feel so damn good, Mara might have worried a little more about why she wasn't able to shut them down before they became a problem for her. She just wasn't sure she wanted to.

"But Victoria's not like any of the women I've been with. I mean, I think I'm kinda into her," Mara confessed, ignoring the doubtful look on Frankie's face. She should have known better than to expect her friend to believe her. She never talked about women like that. "It's weird, I know. I can't explain it. It's all these little things. Like when she laughs, her eyes do this thing where they brighten and then her lashes flutter around them, and there's just genuine joy there. It's one of those contagious laughs, you know? You should have seen us tonight watching *Police Academy*. We laughed so hard it made my abs hurt. And I've seen that movie a hundred times. It was a fresh experience with her. It's just how she is. She makes you feel her joy. She shares it with you. And I know Penny has some kind of issue with her, but you're right, I just couldn't help myself."

Frankie's expression shifted from disbelief to amusement, her lips curling into a knowing smile. "Of course you couldn't. Mara, you only want this woman because you're not supposed to have her. Forbidden fruit tastes the best."

Frankie had a good point. The thought of getting a taste of Victoria caused a stirring in Mara's middle that she couldn't deny. Could it be as simple as the thrill of the chase? Maybe if she just fucked Victoria she would get it out of her system. She would be over it and Penny would never even be the wiser.

"Look, Penny is my best friend. I'm not gonna do anything to screw that up." Mara tucked an unruly curl behind her ear. "I don't want to hurt her over nothing. And one little kiss is definitely nothing. I'll figure out how to handle it with her."

Frankie leaned forward in her seat, interested in getting the whole scoop. "What did Victoria have to say about Penny? Was she weird about you two being friends?"

"Um…" Mara had a sudden and urgent interest in her coffee mug. Anything to avoid the truth of the matter.

"You did tell her you're friends with Penny, right?"

"What's that?"

"Mara!" Frankie stilled both of her hands by pressing them down to the table with her own.

"It didn't come up."

"You have to tell Victoria," Frankie insisted. "And you have to tell Penny you kissed her. Believe me, this is one of those things that's going to get much harder and much, much worse the longer you put it off."

It was true. This was the sort of thing between friends that was best faced head on. Otherwise the lie became the bigger offense than whatever happened in the first place. It was the lie that would poison the friendship, and it would only poison her relationship with Victoria as well.

Relationship? Why would she even think that word? Mara mentally scolded herself. There was no relationship with Victoria to poison. It was one damn kiss, and Mara had made a run for it right after, before things got out of hand. This was not a big deal. She shook her head to clear it and blinked her eyes hard to reset her frame of mind.

"Okay, okay. I'll talk to them." Mara wrapped her hands around the coffee mug in front of her. It had lost its pleasant, piping hot feel.

Frankie was right about telling Penny of course, but one kiss with Victoria didn't necessarily mean there was anything for Mara to lie about. It was only the possibility of good sex that made her go warm at the thought of Victoria, and it wouldn't last past a couple days. There was no sense in starting drama for drama's sake. For now, Mara would keep it under her hat. And as long as Frankie did the same, everything would be fine.

CHAPTER ELEVEN

The next morning, Victoria clutched Mara's green notebook to her side and stood in front of the Rothmoor Tower Casino. She looked up at the grand, gaudy structure, and took a deep breath. Rows and rows of neon lights beckoned people to come play. Mara had to be in there somewhere.

Victoria had spent a restless night tossing and turning with only brief respites of slumber in between. A weird feeling had settled in her stomach the moment Mara had walked out her door, and that feeling had decided to stick around. It wasn't regret that she had kissed her, but rather not knowing why Mara had fled that really ate her up. A "date 'em and dump 'em" reputation was one thing, but Mara had left after just one kiss— one wonderful kiss that had made Victoria's knees weak and her core buzz with desire. By the time the sun came up Victoria had made a decision. She would confront Mara at the casino face-to-face to find out what Mara's deal was. And she would use the notebook Mara had left behind as her excuse for showing up.

As Victoria worked her way through the busy lobby full of people coming and going on a Saturday, she mulled over what to say if she actually did see Mara face-to-face. The obvious choice was a coy, "you left your notebook at my house," but it seemed so hokey. She eyed up the queue for the check-in desk. So many travelers with their suitcases—weekend warriors, high rollers—all too gleefully willing to hand over their hard-earned money for a chance at more. Suddenly it struck her that what she was doing at the casino wasn't much different from them. She was risking something for what was most likely little or no payoff. Only what she was risking wasn't money; it was her dignity. Her face flushed with embarrassing heat and she winced as she recognized the sting of threatening tears in the corners of her eyes. Victoria knew exactly what she would say to Mara. She would tell her to shove her damn dating games and one-night stands. *Womanizer.*

A sharp pain shot through the palm of Victoria's hand. She had tightened her fist into a death grip around the spiral binding of the notebook. She closed her eyes and sucked in a long breath. Surely she looked like a complete idiot standing among the crowd of happy vacationers and hopeful gamblers. This was ridiculous. Victoria didn't need to return the notebook, and she didn't need to analyze Mara's playgirl ways. She could just let it go, chuck the notebook in the nearest garbage bin, and go the hell home.

Victoria spun on her heel and nearly tripped over a bloated backpack a middle-aged man in the line had placed on the floor at his feet. Dancing on tiptoes to regain her balance and not fall completely on her face only increased the embarrassment factor and sweat broke out on her forehead. She mumbled an apology, put her head down, and made a beeline for the exit. She had nearly made it out the door when a familiar voice stopped her in her tracks.

"Victoria? What are you doing here?"

In spite of herself, and the anger she had worked up, Victoria turned and regarded Mara. That beautiful, big smile spread across the comedian's face, her eyes sparkling as if glad—if not genuinely surprised—to see Victoria standing there in the lobby of the Rothmoor. Mara's exposed tanned shoulders and sexy collarbone under the loose-fit, navy blue top she was wearing sent another shot of heat through Victoria's body. She rubbed her face with her free hand and struggled to remember what she had intended to say to Mara. "You…uh…left your notebook at my house," she finally stammered.

For a moment Mara's expression changed to confusion and her eyes travelled down Victoria's body to her outstretched hand offering up the book. The grin returned to Mara's lips. "Oh my god, I totally forgot I'd even taken that with me last night."

What had she expected? Victoria had walked right into playing along. She had said the exact thing she had promised herself she wouldn't. She had acted like a silly girl with an impossible crush and chased Mara—pursued her—even though Mara had bolted after one kiss. She thrust the notebook at her. "You forgot it when you ran out the door. So now you have it back. See ya around."

Victoria meant to storm off quickly, not look back, but it was too late. She saw Mara's happy expression crumble. Mara held the book in front of her, giving it a glum look like she had received a crappy consolation prize. It served Mara right. That was what you got when you played games—a pat on the back and a dismissal from the stage.

"Wait. Don't go." Mara's eyes were full of desperation as her gaze flicked back to Victoria's face. "Listen, I'm sorry about the way I left last night. It's just—"

"Just the way the game goes?" Victoria finished. Blood pounded in her ears as she mentally berated herself for getting into the situation in the first place. This was exactly why she didn't date, and now she was standing in the lobby of a casino arguing about it and looking like a giant fool. She needed to get the hell out of there. Maybe if she was lucky, Maddie would come back into town, take her job back, and Victoria would never even have to see Mara again.

"What game?" Mara's arm dropped to her side and her normally confident posture shifted as her shoulders slumped. "I wasn't playing any game by leaving the notebook with you. I was afraid that…" Her voice trailed off in an exasperated sigh, as if choosing her words carefully. "The only game I played was taking the notebook with me in the first place. I wanted you to see I was serious about planning the fundraiser when we got together. I was prepared to do actual work. Although we worked through the plan together so quickly, I didn't end up writing anything in it."

Mara held out the offending book and flipped through blank page after blank page. "I admit I agreed to the planning session because I really wanted to get to know you. I was interested in you. I…like you. And after last night when we had so much fun together watching the movie, I honestly believed you were into me too. I'm sorry. I should have been more upfront about my motives. I just…I wanted you to give me a chance. I didn't want you to think I was the class clown after that joke I made at the meeting."

Mara gazed at her Vans. She scrunched up her shoulders like she was trying to fold into herself. It was the first time Victoria had ever seen her bravado drop and it melted her heart. Mara was being real with her, and Victoria suspected that wasn't something she did for just anyone. She still hadn't explained why she'd run out the night before, but Mara's earnest expression nudged Victoria into giving her another chance.

Victoria leaned in and spoke in a gentle voice, afraid to break the spell. "I didn't think you were a class clown. And I was definitely into you. But when you ran out on me I just kind of… panicked."

Mara lifted her gaze just in time to meet Victoria's. "I shouldn't have done that. I'm sorry." One corner of her mouth slid up in a smirk and the old Mara was back. "And you have to admit the pussy joke was damn funny."

Even though her voice was low, Victoria still felt a tickle of heat cross her cheeks when Mara said "pussy," but she was not about to let Mara know that it got to her. "Yes, but you should have at least called after leaving like that." She frowned. Mara had started to open up about her feelings before retreating to hide behind her humor again, but she had tipped her hand. Mara had wanted to work with Victoria because she was interested in her. "Tell me more about this interest you have in me." Victoria stuck her chin out, challenging Mara, daring her to open up again.

Mara held her gaze "Do you want me to tell you?" Her left eyebrow arched upward as she moved close enough that her warm breath tickled Victoria's earlobe. "Or do you want me to show you?"

A slow shiver snaked down Victoria's spine and heat pooled between her legs at the mere suggestion. Despite the previous night's experience, sensible reason seemed to slip right out of her brain. She was such a sucker for this woman. "Yes, please."

"Come on." Mara grabbed Victoria's hand and pulled her toward the elevator bay, tossing the notebook in the garbage can after pressing the call button.

"Where are we going?" Victoria's brain buzzed with equal parts curiosity and anticipation.

Mara's gaze was glued to the numbers above the door as if willing the elevator to arrive quickly. "My room."

Suddenly Victoria was wishing for the quick arrival of the elevator as well. What was it about this woman that could make her resolve crumble with just a glance? Anticipation of kissing Mara again flooded her mind while a clench of her heat between her legs threatened to flood her panties. She swallowed hard in an attempt to calm herself. "You have a room here?" She studied Mara's profile. It was just surprise after surprise with this woman.

"I have a suite." Mara squeezed her hand. "I live here."

She followed Mara through the first set of doors, grinning at the urgent way she jabbed at the "close door" button before anyone else could join them in the car. Mara pushed 14 and they stared at the row of numbers above the door until the elevator began its ascent. Victoria felt the upward tug in her belly from the car's movement, and took a slow, calming breath. She had walked in to the Rothmoor to ask a simple question and return a notebook, and instead had ended up on her way to Mara's bed. At least she assumed that was what was happening. The whole shift in mood made her head spin, and the dizzy feeling only added to the adventure.

Suddenly Mara slammed her hand against the emergency stop on the control panel. She faced Victoria, quickly backing her up against the wall. Pressing against her, Mara kissed her, first brushing her lips softly against hers—once…twice, then the third time more firmly and urgently.

Damn. Elevator sex. This would be a first for her. Another wave of excitement washed over her as she tangled her fingers in Mara's hair, encouraging the trail she made down her neck. It was a mistake. She was falling for Mara's charms again. Look where that had landed her the other night. Her brain tried to convince the rest of her body to put a stop to it, but it felt so damn good.

Mara had just slipped her hands under her tank top and found the lace of her bra when a disembodied voice crackled through a speaker overhead. "Mara, is everything okay in there?"

Victoria gasped, realizing that the voice had identified Mara by name. Did Mara have a reputation for stopping elevators like that? It would fit with the womanizer description Maddie had warned her about. She *had* run out on her and hadn't even bothered to call. It was somewhat suspicious, even if Mara's warm breath on Victoria's skin was giving her a dizzying rush that made her knees go weak.

"It's okay. That's just Scott the security guy," Mara murmured against Victoria's neck, not missing a beat, before shouting, "We're fine Scott, thanks."

Mara's fingertips freed her breasts from the cups of her bra, and her breath hitched again as her traitorous nipples went hard at the touch.

The interruption was a sign—a sign that Victoria should stop it right now before she jumped into her bed and ended up burned and broken. The morning after a kiss was bad enough. After sex? That could do her in for good. She opened her mouth to say as much, but the speaker crackled again.

"You can't just stop an elevator like that. For your own personal use…or whatever." The voice—Scott—sighed in exasperation over the static of the connection.

"Okay. Roger that," Mara mumbled. She didn't seem deterred by the warning at all as she slid her tongue along Victoria's collarbone and completely disregarded the reprimand. "Ten-four."

According to Victoria's brain, now would be the time to speak up. The other parts of her pulsing so desperately to be touched seemed to block the words from making it to her lips. She didn't want to stop. She wanted every last bit of Mara. Consequences be damned.

"Mara. There's a camera in there. I can see you," Scott said.

Mara stopped kissing Victoria with a frustrated half-moan, half-growl and reached out to release the emergency stop. "Fine!"

"Thank you." The speaker crackled off and the car continued its journey to the fourteenth floor.

Victoria sucked in a deep breath to cool her arousal. Get it together. "I'm guessing you know him?" It was interesting that the guy had said anything at all instead of just letting the incident slide. Almost as if he enjoyed busting on Mara.

"Yep. Don't worry about Scott. He's friends with…" Mara trailed off, shutting her eyes and shaking her head. "He's a friend."

It seemed like Mara had skipped over something she was going to say. He's friends with…*who*? She opened her mouth to ask a follow up question, but the elevator dinged and the doors opened before she had the chance.

Mara's eyes sparkled as she raised her eyebrows and bit her lip. Totally sexy. "We'll just continue this inside." She took her hand and led her down the corridor.

Victoria followed, too drawn in by the temptation of finding out what was really going on between her and Mara to back out. She might have blissfully continued in the sex fog of the moment if she hadn't caught a glimpse of the big "R" of the Rothmoor insignia on the elevator door when it closed behind them. Suddenly thoughts of her sister's warnings about Mara popped back into her head. *She's a total playgirl. Definitely not the kind you're going to pin down and mold into the perfect girlfriend.*

Suddenly her stomach lurched. This was a mistake—all if it. Showing up at the Rothmoor, following Mara to her room. Victoria didn't need the complication in her life. She needed to do what she had promised to do for Maddie—represent Emerald Isle until her sister's return—and then leave all this behind and go on with her quiet, peaceful life. A date for her grandmother's party was not worth the heartbreak that would no doubt ensue.

Somehow she was going to have to find the strength to resist Mara's charm and stick to it. It was Victoria's turn to make a hasty retreat and run off like Mara had after the kiss the night before. Much easier said than done, she realized as Mara gave her a wink and ushered her into the suite.

CHAPTER TWELVE

Mara pulled Victoria into her suite and shut the door firmly behind them. Privacy, at last. Time to see if all she needed was to get this woman out of her system and see if one delicious roll in the sheets would quell the fiery need that had taken over her when they were in the elevator together. She slid her hand from Victoria's wrist to her hip as she pinned her against the door. Their lips were a fraction of an inch from making contact. Anticipation of the kiss caused a surge of heat through Mara's middle. "Now, where did we leave off?"

Victoria's previously caught-off-guard, wide-eyed expression softened with a flutter of her eyelids, and her mouth opened. As their lips pressed together, she dug her fingertips into Mara's shoulders, encouraging her kiss.

Mara probed her tongue boldly between Victoria's lips, eliciting a low moan from her, but suddenly the spell was broken. The hands that had just been pulling Mara in and urging her on, were now flat palms pushing her away as Victoria broke off the kiss.

"Wait," she gasped. "Stop."

Stop? Mara instinctively took a step back and released her hold on Victoria's hips. She wasn't used to women telling her to stop, but she certainly didn't want to steamroll over consent. Her heart pounded as she studied Victoria, who was hiding her face in her hands.

"Hey." Mara's tone was gentle as she pulled Victoria's hands down. "I'm sorry. Did you not want me to kiss you?"

Her mind raced to reconcile the rollercoaster of emotions she had experienced in the twenty minutes before that moment. First the surprise of seeing Victoria in the lobby of the Rothmoor. Then there was the embarrassment of rehashing her great escape the night before and the moment that she believed Victoria was angry enough to walk out on her. When they finally sorted that out and ended up in the elevator together, it was all Mara could do to keep her hands off Victoria. If Scott hadn't cut in on them, Mara would have fucked her right then and there and she was certain Victoria would have been okay with it. So what was with the sudden one-eighty?

Victoria shook her head and cleared her throat as if trying to find her voice. "No. I mean, yes." She closed her eyes and took a deep breath. "I mean yes, I did very much want you to kiss me."

"But?"

"But I also wanted you to stop."

Mara turned to the bar cart next to the television and Victoria followed. "I think I need a drink."

"I'm sorry. I know I'm not making any sense. I did want you to kiss me. I still do. It's just…" Victoria hesitated and took another deep breath. That couldn't be a good sign. Mara poured a whiskey while Victoria said, "You have a reputation as a womanizer and I'm not interested in being one of your flings."

"A reputation as a what?" Mara spun around quickly but misjudged how close they were. She watched in horror as the liquid in her glass splashed onto Victoria's white shirt. The amber stain spread quickly down the front of the fabric. "Oh fuck. I'm sorry."

Nothing about this was okay. Mara was never this clumsy around women. Women never turned her down. She never gave this much of a damn about what anyone thought of her, but yet somehow here she was—cheeks hot with embarrassment and hoping Victoria didn't slap her across the face and tell her to fuck all the way off.

Victoria's mouth opened and shut, but no sounds came out as she assessed the damage. Her white tank top was now sheer with wetness, shellacked by the whiskey to her skin.

"You should rinse that out before it's ruined." Mara set her empty glass back down and waved in the direction of her bathroom. "Go ahead and wash up. I'll get you a fresh shirt."

Victoria nodded numbly and peeled her shirt from her body as she ambled down the short hallway.

Before Mara could make good on the promise of a dry shirt, there was a knock on the front door.

"Mara? Are you in there? Open up."

Penny. And she had her "manager boss lady" voice on. Perfect fucking timing. Mara hadn't had the chance to revisit the subject of Victoria McHenry with Penny since the kiss the night before, and something told her that now wasn't the optimal time to bring it up.

Mara opened the door just a crack and peeked out at her best friend. "Penny! What's going on?"

"I know I keep saying there are lines we shouldn't cross, but Ricky Jenkins just…" Her voice trailed off and she stuck her hand in the door to push it open a bit more and get a better look into the suite, more interested in nosing into Mara's business then telling her story. "Is your water running?"

"Isn't that a line from a prank call?" Mara countered, stalling. As interested as she was in hearing what Penny had to say about Ricky Jenkins, the headliner at the Laffmoor, she couldn't let Penny know Victoria was there.

Penny's eyes went wide with sudden realization. "Oh my god, you have a girl here! Who is it?"

She hated to lie to Penny, but this was definitely not the time to bring up the fact that she had a half-naked Victoria in her bathroom whom she had planned to get it on with. But there was a chance Victoria wasn't going to be sticking around much longer due to the whiskey-soaked tank top fiasco. So, no. There was no good reason to discuss Victoria and what may or may not be happening between the two of them with Penny.

"What? No." Mara blocked Penny from completely barging into the suite. "I don't kiss and tell."

Penny put her hands on her hips and stared at Mara defiantly. "Since when? Come on, tell me!"

Womanizer. Victoria's accusation echoed in Mara's head. Was she a womanizer? Was that why her friends had been on her case about settling down recently? *No.* Mara didn't have time for a relationship. That wasn't a crime. She needed to sort things out with Victoria, and that meant she needed to send Penny on her way. She had to redirect the conversation and fast. Victoria had already been in the bathroom for a while, and if she didn't produce a fresh shirt soon, there was a chance Victoria would come looking for her. A change of subject was the best she could do. "No. Now, what happened with Jenkins?"

"What? Oh, Ricky." Penny's face fell as if remembering her original objective for showing up at the door, and Mara felt bad for taking away her distraction. "It was stupid. I'm probably overreacting, and I really shouldn't say anything anyway. Go back to your lady-friend and forget about it."

"Penny, are you sure?" A wave of relief washed over Mara. If something were seriously wrong, Penny would just come out and say it. They were best friends. They were on that level.

"Yeah, I'm good." Penny waved a hand like she was batting her troubles away. "No big deal."

Suddenly the water running in the bathroom cut off which meant Victoria would be coming out of the bathroom and the disaster of Victoria and Penny colliding socially was mere seconds away. Penny was about to see a topless Victoria strolling through the suite if Mara didn't shut the damn door. She had no choice but to cut the visit short.

"Okay, great! Glad you're good. We'll definitely catch up later." Her voice inched up higher and higher as the words tumbled out, until it was like a recording on fast forward. Penny frowned with bewilderment as Mara shut the door on her.

"Mara, do you have that shirt for me?" Victoria emerged from the bathroom just as the door to the suite clicked into place. She was completely adorable, modestly holding her wet tank in front of her bra to cover up.

"Sure thing." Mara raced to make up for the time she'd spent talking to Penny and yanked an old Miami U T-shirt from her drawer. "This should do the trick." She politely averted her eyes as Victoria tugged the dry shirt over her head.

"So, what were you saying?" Victoria asked.

Victoria ran her hands down her front in an attempt to brush out the wrinkles from a shirt that had been balled up in Mara's drawer for at least three weeks, an apparent effort to still appear dignified and elegant while wearing a bright orange shirt with a hole in the shoulder.

Mara recalled damn well what she had been saying, and she suspected Victoria did too. She had been defending herself against the same message she had heard repeatedly over the past week. Frankie calling her a player, Penny asking her if she would ever settle down, and now Victoria advising her that she had earned herself a reputation as a womanizer. It was all total bullshit. Wasn't it? She was perfectly capable of having a relationship with someone. She just hadn't wanted to. That was still true. She didn't want a relationship, but she wasn't exactly ready to watch Victoria walk out on her just yet either.

"I was saying, I'm not a womanizer. That's not fair at all. That term implies the other party doesn't know what they're getting into. I never made any promises to anyone, and they made none to me." Mara frowned. Saying it out loud like that did make it sound sad. "Anyway, it works."

"I'm not asking you for any promises either." Victoria sounded calmer than she had since they bumped into each other in the lobby. It was like a whole new woman had emerged from the bathroom. Maybe being splashed with that drink was exactly what she needed to cool down. She walked over to the sofa and plopped down on the overstuffed cushion.

Mara felt relief wash over her. If Victoria was sitting down, especially with the way she was tucking her feet under her, she wasn't planning on running out the door any time soon. This was certainly a turn of events from the dead stop Victoria had put on their making out when they first entered the suite.

Mara cautiously perched on the far arm of the sofa. "So what are you asking for?"

Victoria chewed her bottom lip as if actually considering the question. "How about an actual date?"

"I don't date." The automatic response was out of her suddenly dry mouth before she could stop it. A knee-jerk reaction. Or at least a jerk reaction. No wonder she was gaining a reputation. Maybe she really wasn't capable of being in a relationship. She was allergic to them or something.

Victoria didn't stand, but she untucked her feet and plopped them down as if she was suddenly uncomfortable. "Of course not. I'm sorry." She shook her head. "Coming here was clearly a mistake."

Mara's heart sank at the prospect of Victoria leaving. She had to say something to stop her. Something. Anything. "I don't usually date, but I could."

She could date. In theory. There was nothing stopping her. She just didn't do it. She didn't know what had made her say that she could. It was the first thing that popped into her mind when she thought Victoria was going to walk out on her. In that moment Mara would have said anything to keep her on the couch. Maybe she was coming down with something. That was it. She was sick.

"You *could?*" Victoria's lips slid into an amused smile.

Once again heat crept into Mara's cheeks and behind her ears. She had the urge to laugh off her embarrassment, make her body's response no big deal, but that didn't seem like it would help the situation. Instead she slid down from the arm of the sofa onto the cushion next to Victoria. Damn she wanted to kiss that smart smile right off her lips. "I mean I could date if the right person came along." Her voice came out huskier than she intended. Merely sitting close to Victoria dressed in her old threadbare T-shirt was causing a dizzying lust to fog her brain.

"My god, are you coming on to me right now?" Victoria shook her head, but her smile remained fixed on her face. "Mara, I like you, and the kiss and the stuff in the elevator was…very, very good. But I don't want to be one of your flings."

Mara sighed, her pride wounded. It always came back to that. "So you want to date?"

Victoria scooted back in her seat, making herself a little taller and more poised. "No. I want a date. I need a date for my grandmother's birthday party. If I show up solo, my mother will attempt to set me up with every single man in the Las Vegas area." She paused and Mara took the opportunity to roll her eyes to match the dramatics of the statement. Victoria quickly corrected herself. "Okay. With every single man in the ballroom that night. My mother isn't exactly on board with my dating preferences. She thinks I just haven't met the right jet setter. She reminds me every chance she gets. I came out when I was in college, but she remains convinced it's a phase. It's exhausting. So, I'd like to spare myself the grief. The best way to do that is to take a date to the party."

"I would be that date," Mara mused. The old pretend girlfriend trick. Not a bad gig, although in this case it would mean some intense familial scrutiny. She liked Victoria and certainly wouldn't mind spending some time with her. Plus, if she played this right, maybe she could get her friends off her back about her not wanting a relationship. She would just have to have a little chat with Penny and tell her to get over the past. People could change. That was exactly the point she was trying to make. Struck with inspiration, she formulated a counter-offer. "I will be that date but I'm gonna need something from you."

"Don't say sex."

"Ha, ha." Mara stuck her tongue out before continuing with her plan. "I was actually going to say I will be your date for the party, but you have to date me from now until then."

Victoria squinted suspiciously from her side of the couch. "I have to date you?"

"From now until then," Mara confirmed with a nod. The idea was really picking up steam in her mind. She would hang out with Victoria for the next few weeks, fake date and be seen around town with her new girlfriend and prove to her friends that she was perfectly capable of being in a relationship. After the birthday party they could fake break up and go on with their lives. It was brilliant. "What do you say?"

"I'm not going to sleep with you." Victoria crossed her arms defiantly, but the way her eyebrow slid up made the statement seem like a direct challenge to Mara.

"Of course not." Mara winked. "There's just one thing we should probably discuss before this goes any further. Penny Rothmoor is my best friend."

Victoria winced at the name, verifying that there was, as Penny had stated, a past there. She recovered quickly and a pleasant smile returned to her lips. "I went to high school with Penny."

Okay. Apparently no one was giving up the story. "Then, you're cool with her?"

"I haven't even seen her since we were teenagers, but we were kind of friends back then. For a while." Victoria shrugged. "Why? Did she say something about me?"

Mara shook her head. "No. Only that she knew you from years ago." She clearly wasn't going to get the full scoop, but as long as her best friend and fake girlfriend could be in the same room without coming to blows because of their mysterious past, she could live with that. They were all adults now. The teenage drama could be left in the past.

"Good. Then that's settled." The look of relief was evident on Victoria's face. "We're dating."

"We're dating," Mara repeated.

The deal was sealed.

CHAPTER THIRTEEN

Mara sat at her usual table in Café Gato with Singe the cat on her lap. She squinted as the morning sun streamed through the big window and sipped her coffee, enjoying the bewildered look on Frankie's face.

"Let me get this straight. You're…dating Victoria McHenry?" Frankie shook her head and her curls bounced around joyfully in spite of her scolding tone. "Mmm-hmm. You do know that sleeping with a woman and leaving in the middle of the night does not constitute dating, right?"

"That's not what happened at all, Frankie. If you must know, I haven't even slept with her yet. She came over and we had a really good talk and we actually like each other. We decided to give it a go."

She had woken up with a buzz in her chest, a humming that had started at the prospect of announcing to her friends that she was dating someone that had developed into a life-carrying force driving her through her day. The sun was shining brighter than normal. The usual din of conversation in the café was a chipper chatter of patrons enjoying a delicious cup of coffee, their voices almost like a song. The fact that this mood was built completely on a fiction that she and Victoria had created the day before in her suite in the casino... Well, she was content to push that part from her brain for now. Instead, she would ride the wave while it lasted.

Frankie frowned. "So you talked through the uncomfortable past with both of them?"

She drained the last of the coffee and dabbed at her mouth with a napkin. She still hadn't totally worked out how she was going to handle the Penny part. "Not both of them, but I told Victoria I'm friends with Penny and she was okay with it. I promise I'll talk to Penny too."

"And this isn't another one of your love 'em and leave 'em things?" Frankie still looked doubtful.

"No, I'm serious. I like her." It wasn't a lie. Mara did like Victoria. Sure, the "dating" thing had come in a little more manufactured way than an organic one, but Victoria had agreed to date her for the next few weeks. So it was the truth. They were dating. "And you guys are gonna like her too."

"Just promise you're going to talk to Penny soon."

"I think I already said that I would."

Fortunately, the bell above the door chimed putting an end to the conversation. Jenna and Hayleigh came into the cafe, a cake box balanced in Jenna's arms.

"Check it out!" Jenna placed the flat box on their table. "The birthday girl is ready to party."

Mara peeked through the cellophane top and saw a bright pink flowered cake with the message "Happy Birthday Hayleigh" scrawled in icing. "Hey, happy birthday!" She smiled brightly at Hayleigh, relieved for the interruption. Something in the way Frankie had looked at her gave Mara a queasy twinge in her stomach, but now the heat was off her. At least for the moment.

"Blah," Hayleigh said, plopping into the chair next to Mara, her long, tanned dancer legs clad in short shorts sprawled comfortably under the table. Upon closer inspection, the birthday girl didn't look totally ready to party. She seemed glum and a bit harried. "Another birthday just means another year older."

Mara flicked her gaze from Frankie to Jenna. The rest of the group all had at least three years on Hayleigh. She was the baby of the bunch. Hayleigh was in no way older or even oldish. Hell, she wasn't even that mature for a twenty-something.

"What's wrong, honey?" Frankie asked. She slipped naturally into her role as mother hen in the group. "Aren't you excited about tonight?"

"Oh, she's all about the party." Jenna stood behind her girlfriend and squeezed her shoulders. "It's the number twenty-five that's got her down. She's being ridiculous."

Hayleigh was being ridiculous. Besides having the body that came with a lifetime of dance classes, she had that All-American girl next door look—blond hair and blue eyes. The perfect Vegas showgirl look. Unfortunately, Hayleigh just hadn't had her big break yet.

Mara nodded reassuringly in agreement. "You're a youngster. Fresh-faced as ever. No worries."

"You guys don't get it. I'm a dancer. Twenty-five is old. And I still haven't made it here," Hayleigh pouted. "I'm practically over the hill. I *am* Las Vegas over the hill."

"Oh girl, you are not over the hill." Frankie dismissed Hayleigh's laments with a wave of her hand. "You are not even close to the hill. You're so far away from it, you would need binoculars just to see the hill."

"I think she gets it," Mara murmured.

Frankie shot Mara a stern look and said, "As I was saying, you'll reach your dreams. You just have to keep pushing forward. Look at you now! I bet you're one of the best bar-top dancers in town!"

"Yeah, that's probably not helping, Frankie." Jenna slid into an empty chair while Frankie gave a somewhat sheepish shrug. "Anyway, we're not worrying about any of that shit tonight. Tonight we party. Nine o'clock, Game of Flats—be there."

"And stay there," Hayleigh chimed in, looking pointedly at Mara. "What the hell happened to you the other night? I thought you were going to hang out with me at Flats."

"Oh, she left with her new woman," Frankie volunteered, obviously still put off by the other women shutting down her cheer-up campaign. "They're *dating* now."

Hayleigh leaned forward in her seat, resting her chin atop her fists, waiting for her friend to dish. "What woman?"

Mara shook her head. "Don't do that."

A youthful energy had returned to Hayleigh as she perked up and gave Mara the Miss Middle-America innocent eyes. She even batted her lashes to seal the deal. "Do what?"

"That thing where you hunker down like Barbara Walters going in for the celebrity gossip kill." Mara drained the last of the coffee in her mug. "I've met someone. We're…dating."

There. She had said it herself, out loud in front of the group. She was dating someone and the world around her hadn't imploded. Mara had managed to utter the words that only two days before she thought would never cross her lips.

"Are you bringing this woman to the party tonight?" Jenna asked. "I'm sure we would all like to meet her."

There it was, the big chance to show up with actual proof that she was in a relationship and not just talking out of her ass. Showtime. Taking someone along to a club was not a big deal, and yet Mara's gut did a total summersault at the thought of taking Victoria. First of all, there was the potential of in-depth interrogation by her friends. No doubt Victoria would hold up her end of the bargain and play along, but it could very well be an exhausting night for the fake couple. Secondly, there was the fact that Mara still hadn't talked to Penny. Although she wasn't actually sleeping with Victoria, by declaring in front of all her friends that they were dating, everyone would assume they were. Mara couldn't just blindside her best friend with this information at Hayleigh's party. It wouldn't be right. Mara was just going to have to suck it up and tell Penny.

"Mara." Hayleigh snapped her fingers impatiently to bring her back into focus. "Are you bringing the chick or what?"

"Absolutely," Mara confirmed with a stiff nod that she hoped conveyed more confidence than her still-roiling insides were ready to concede. "We can't come until after my set, but you will meet her tonight."

CHAPTER FOURTEEN

Chimes and dings from the slot machines filled the air as Mara walked across the casino floor of the Rothmoor. Somewhere to her left an electric version of *The Price Is Right* theme song screamed, beckoning to gamblers who hadn't yet spent all their nickels. Mara loved the buzz and hum of the floor even in the middle of the day.

After the afternoon comedy show was over, she always liked to make at least one full lap of the casino floor. Sometimes she was recognized by someone who had been in the audience, and occasionally she even signed an autograph or two. It was great for the ego. On top of that, people watching in the casino was excellent. Half of the crowd was on a gambling high, trying to extend their run of good luck. The other half was full of desperate hope—sure that one more spin would be the big one.

She rounded the corner past the roulette tables and finally spotted Penny standing at the end of the bar, waiting for the bartender. Penny was picking at her manicure and trying to get her end-of-shift work completed. She was distracted. It was the perfect time for Mara to say what she had been wanting to say to her best friend.

"Hey, Penny!" Mara called, attempting a bright smile. "I'm glad I ran into you. I wanted to talk to you about…something."

"What?" Penny's eyes went wide. It must have been a hard shift. She looked dazed like she was worn out and struggling to stay alert. "Did something happen at the show? Oh god, what happened?"

"No, I mean…" Mara had to get it out. It was like Frankie advised, the sooner she got it over with, the better. She slid onto the barstool next to Penny, making herself comfortable for what could be a rough conversation, and cleared her throat. "I mean, I have to tell you something about me."

"Go on." Penny perked up enough to turn her full attention to Mara. "Is this about your mystery lady?"

Rip the band aid off.

"As a matter of fact, it is." Mara took a deep breath and then just let the words out. "I've been working with Victoria McHenry on the fundraiser for the Animal Shelter and we've gotten to know each other, and we really click and now I'm dating her."

She expected some kind of reaction from Penny. A scream, a laugh, a level five explosion, like when staff did something stupid during her shift managing the floor. But instead all Mara got was a blank stare. In a way it was even scarier than a level five.

"Huh. Okay."

"I didn't know this was going to happen when we talked the other day at lunch. I didn't expect this. But here we are," Mara said. "I know you two have some kind of past that apparently nobody wants to talk about, but I have to at least know that you'll be okay if I bring her around every once and a while."

"Bring her around?" Penny tapped her pen against her clipboard. She was distracted. "Oh yeah. Bring her around. I'm okay with it."

"I know you think this is weird. I'm sorry."

"You have nothing to apologize for, and I don't think it's weird." Penny dropped her clipboard onto the bar, sending the pen she had been holding skittering across the surface. She sighed and took a beat to compose herself. "I'm really okay with it."

"Are you sure? Because I'm bringing her to Hayleigh's party with me tonight."

"Nothing like jumping right in," Penny said flatly before closing her eyes and drawing in a big breath. A calming measure.

"You don't seem okay."

"I am. Really." Penny pinched the bridge of her nose. "It's just that I know how these things go for you. I've seen it before, only this time it's a woman I know. Victoria will be the girl du jour. You'll be all hot and heavy, and then it will be out of your system and you'll be over her and on to the next woman. It's just your thing. But Victoria's an adult. If she makes the decision to be with you, that's on her. It's not my business."

"That is not my thing." Prickly, uncomfortable heat creeped up Mara's neck and the words, "*Play on, playa*" in Frankie's chanting voice danced around in the back of her mind. It had never bothered Mara before that her friends thought she treated other girls that way, but somehow talking about Victoria in that context made her blood boil.

This was how Mara's friends saw her. This was her reputation, and everyone had accepted that. But no more. Now they would see her dating Victoria, see that she could be in a relationship if she really wanted to be, and she would be free of the bad rap.

"No," Mara insisted. "This isn't that. I'm serious with Victoria. It's not a fling."

"Okay, Mara." Penny's voice took on a slightly sarcastic, fully patronizing tone. "Then I assume you broke off things with Kat?"

Kat? Mara had actually forgotten all about Kat, her friend the chef, coming into town. "I didn't, but I will. Tomorrow. It's the middle of dinner rush in New York right now."

"Sure you will. It doesn't matter to me." Penny had pulled herself up to her full, high-heeled height and was standing with her hands balled in fists on her hips, challenging Mara.

"Fine. I'll do it now." Mara pulled her phone from her back pocket and started furiously thumb-typing an, "I've met someone" message to Kat. Halfway through she glanced up to stick her tongue out childishly at Penny.

"Hey, you do whatever you want about Kat. I was just making a point," Penny said gathering her belongings. "I gotta run. Lauren's flight is due in about thirty minutes and I'm meeting her at the airport. We'll see you—and Victoria—at the party tonight."

Without waiting for Mara to react, Penny took off faster than one would think her stilettos could carry her after being on her feet all day. Lauren's imminent return had obviously put some pep in Penny's step. The message Mara was typing to Kat could have waited and Penny would never be the wiser, but it needed to be done anyway. If she was dating Victoria, she would be all in. Mara completed the text and pressed send.

It was nearly ten thirty when the fake couple finally arrived at the club. Mara pushed through the doors of Game of Flats ready to celebrate Hayleigh's twenty-fifth birthday with her friends, and of course, her new girlfriend. Victoria had seemed a little nervous when they met up in the lobby of the casino, but hand in hand they were ready to take on the world, or at least the dreaded lesbian friend circle.

The smoky club was already throbbing with loud music and a crammed dance floor. Mara spotted the birthday girl dancing on the bar with Jenna. Hayleigh looked much more like her usual self than she had earlier in the day. Her outfit was striking on her tall body—short black shorts and a red sequined halter, knee-high boots clacking along as she crossed the bar top. Around her neck hung several strands of what looked like Mardi Gras beads, but in every color of the rainbow. There was no doubt she was the star of this show. Below the couple, standing at the bar, was the rest of their group. Mara pushed her way through the crowd to join them. Hayleigh and Jenna both climbed down off the bar as she approached and greeted her with a hug.

"You brought your special lady!" Hayleigh giggled, already tipsy.

Mara tried not to flinch as she flicked her gaze over to Penny. Their conversation had ended so abruptly that afternoon and Mara still wasn't sure how Penny would react when she actually saw the couple in person. But it appeared her best friend hadn't even heard Hayleigh. Penny appeared to be deep in conversation with Lauren, the lovebirds totally lost in their own little world.

"I did," Mara grinned. "This is Victoria McHenry."

Mara introduced Victoria to the gang and everyone said hello, and thankfully, did not act that stunned that Mara had shown up with a date. It had to have been an awkward enough situation for Victoria, although she appeared to have the grace and poise to handle herself. She even shared a somewhat friendly, although brief, exchange with Penny and Lauren. Mara was relieved that her best friend was too distracted for a full-on high school reunion, but she was happy for her too. She knew the long-distance relationship thing was hard on Penny, but any time Lauren came back into town and they were together again, it was like all of that stress just melted away.

"Come on, you guys. It's my party and I want to dance!" Hayleigh linked an arm through Mara's and pulled her toward the dance floor. On the way she grabbed Penny and towed her and Lauren along as well.

Once out in the middle of the crowd, the six women made a tight circle, dancing to the beat pumping through the club. Hayleigh danced up on Jenna, who bobbed her head in time with the music, her expression smug and clearly proud of the attention her girlfriend lavished upon her. Victoria fit right in with the rest of them, and to Mara's delight, she honestly seemed to be enjoying herself. Even Penny began to let loose, waving her arms in the air, giving in to the mob mentality of the dance floor.

Mara's gaze flicked over to the DJ, the same popular girl from the other night, her booth surrounded by another bunch of groupies. "Hey." She leaned closer to Frankie to be heard. "That chick is eyeing you up."

"What? Who?" Frankie looked over her shoulder like maybe she was being followed.

"The DJ." Mara tipped her head in the direction she wanted Frankie to point her gaze. "She was watching you."

As Frankie lifted her head toward the direction of the booth, the DJ bit her lip, then quickly looked away. Busted.

"No way. You're nuts."

"She was," Mara insisted.

Frankie turned her back to the booth and reapplied her energy to her dance moves. "Besides she's not my type. I like someone more like…like her."

Mara followed Frankie's focus to a girl dancing just outside of their group's circle. Long brown hair, simple olive-green tank top and wide-leg jeans that grazed the floor and almost completely covered her flip flops. The long, glass-beaded necklaces draped around her neck looked just like something Frankie would wear. Au natural, earth mother, trippy-dippy granola types. As much as Mara loved her friend, after dating Frankie she had crossed that "type" off her list of potential girlfriend material. As far as Mara was concerned, there was such a thing as "too laid back."

"Talk to her for me, Mara." Frankie grabbed her wrist and gave it an encouraging squeeze. "Please, please, please."

"Come on, no. I am not playing wing ma'am tonight. I have a date!" Mara wiggled out of Frankie's grasp and scooted closer to Victoria. As she did, the target of Frankie's admiration caught them looking and danced her way over. Mara looked to Penny for back up, but her best friend was preoccupied bumping and grinding with her girlfriend. At least Penny was finally relaxing and having fun. Lauren was a miracle worker.

"Hey, do I know you? You look familiar." The mystery dancer cut in between Mara and Victoria.

"I don't think so." Mara shook her head and attempted to redirect the girl. "But maybe you know my friend, Frankie?"

Fortunately Frankie took the opportunity and the girl's attention off Mara. "Hi. That's me. I'm Frankie."

"Blu." The girl flashed Frankie a winning smile and easily fell into dancing beside her.

With her friends all paired up, Mara directed her attention to Victoria. The redhead moved in time to the music with a casual, natural style that showed this was not her first time out. When she did a double spin mid-move without missing a beat, Mara let out a whoop of admiration.

"You're a natural." She beamed at her date. "I had no idea you had moves like that."

"It's not all that natural," Victoria confessed. "My mother insisted on tap and ballet lessons twice a week from first through eighth grade. Believe me, I've still got the callouses to prove it."

"I guess moms are just programmed to want us to learn something," Mara shrugged. "Yours pushed dance. Mine pushed cooking."

"You can cook?" It was Victoria's turn to look impressed.

"Yeah, but…" Mara shook her head at the absurdity of them trying to hold a conversation in the middle of the dance floor. It would be much easier to communicate away from the crowd. She led Victoria to a tall cocktail table against the far wall opposite the bar. "Yes, I can cook, but it's still nothing compared to my mom. She makes a lasagna so good you'll want to name your firstborn child after her."

Victoria's eyes lit up. "Oh my god, lasagna is my absolute favorite. My mother never served food like that when we were growing up. Dinners were elaborate salads, or on the rare occasions that my father joined us for a meal, lean cuts of meat and loads of veggies. All made by our cook."

"That sounds amazingly boring," Mara laughed. She couldn't imagine a family meal without delicious breads and all the fixings. "Although perhaps it was appropriate for your dance training regime."

"No, just boring." Victoria smiled and her eyes sparkled as she joined in on the joke. "But once I got out of that house and discovered the joys of pasta, there was no turning back."

"The joy of pasta—you have no idea." There were pasta dishes, and then there were Antoinette Antonini pasta dishes. Her mom could cook like no one else. It was a point of pride for her. Mara reached across the tabletop and brushed her fingertips across the back of Victoria's hand. She wanted to share the experience of her mother's cooking with her. If Victoria loved a good lasagna, she would be blown away by Antoinette's. "Listen, my mom is coming to visit next week on her way to go see her sister in California. She's only here for one night, but she always cooks for me when she comes. You can come over to my place and I'll have her make us lasagna. You will not regret it."

Victoria jerked her hand away and pulled it to her beautiful lips. "I couldn't possibly intrude on your visit with your mother like that. You should spend that time with her. You barely even know me."

The irony of going from someone who didn't date to introducing a woman to her mom, after only a few days of knowing each other, wasn't lost on Mara. But if there was one thing she had learned from her family, it was that a good meal was best shared with others, whether it be new friends or old. "Of course you can. If we're going to pull off this pretend dating thing, we better get used to one another. I mean, we may as well be friends, right?"

The surprise on Victoria's face melted into an expression of relief, and the smile returned to her lips as she dropped her hand back onto the table, connecting once again with Mara's. "You're right. How could I possibly pass up the chance to try Mrs. Antonini's famous lasagna? I'm in."

"Perfect."

Convincing Victoria to join her for dinner felt like a victory. It had to be the old thrill of the chase and not Victoria grabbing onto her hand again that filled her with a sudden warmth. It was just the small win and the chance to brag about her mom's home cooking that made her pulse race. Nothing more.

Luckily, before she could put too fine a point on it, Frankie came bounding up to their table. "Hey, lovebirds." She put a hand on each of their shoulders and gave a squeeze to match each syllable in lovebirds. "Hayleigh's about to cut the cake. Come on."

They followed Frankie to the back of the club where a group of tables had been pushed together. They smiled politely while the birthday girl gave a brief, yet dramatic speech lamenting her old age. In the spirit of birthday generosity, her friends did their best to indulge Hayleigh and not roll their eyes at her ridiculousness. Most of them had enough alcohol in them to forgive her youthful folly. They all sang as the twenty-five year old blew out her candles.

Mara grinned and wrapped an arm around Victoria's waist as they watched Hayleigh cut the cake and the crowd cheered. Date one with Victoria was on the books and date two was set. Maybe she was good at the dating thing after all.

CHAPTER FIFTEEN

The next morning, Victoria stood in the nurses' station leaning against the edge of the built-in desk. She had spent the first part of her shift running from room to room tending to patients, and she was grateful for a two-minute break to catch her breath and think about things—or overthink things, which was exactly what she was doing.

It was weird that she hadn't given Penny Rothmoor a thought in almost fifteen years, and yet here the woman was, popping up out of the blue, haunting Victoria's conscience. Victoria hadn't given Penny a thought mostly because she had made an effort to block all thoughts of Penny from her mind. It hadn't been easy at first, but she had trained her brain. She'd had to.

Victoria and Penny had been the closest of friends during the fall of their senior year of high school. They had attended school together for years, but it wasn't until the twelfth grade when Penny was full of teenage angst and a drive to rebel against the family business that the two had bonded. Of course, since then Penny's viewpoint had changed, but back then it was endless irony and jokes about the over-the-top extravagance, heinous wastefulness, and pathetic suckers emptying their pockets for an impossible dream.

Then one night, Victoria and Penny were doing their usual—sitting on top of a picnic table, laughing about some ridiculously overpriced dinner event their parents had attended the weekend prior, scoffing at the price tags of their mothers' dresses and questioning the list of semi-celebrities who were rumored to have been in attendance. They talked about how they were going to live life so differently once they graduated and got out into the real world. Then something happened and everything changed.

Just as Victoria was saying she wanted a career in a field that would make a difference in the world, launching into her hopes and dreams and her vision for the future, Penny leaned in and kissed her squarely on the lips. Much more than a friendly peck. And Victoria had liked it. A lot. And it freaked her out. A lot. Victoria made some lame excuse as to why she had to leave right that very minute. Poor Penny just sat and watched her go.

After that night in the park, Victoria kept her distance from Penny. She avoided her in the halls at school and stopped returning her calls. She bailed out. Their friendship just evaporated into nothingness, very much the same way Victoria had run off into the darkness of the park. They never even spoke again, not for lack of trying on Penny's part. But Victoria kept her head down and avoided facing her, as well as the feelings she had when kissing a girl.

In hindsight, Victoria saw the events of that evening in a whole different light. Of course, she understood the feelings she discovered that night more and more as time passed. But it wasn't regret or disappointment that pinged and tickled around her brain when she thought back on it. She regretted the way she handled the situation and hurt a friend. Penny had taught Victoria something about herself, and Victoria was ashamed of the way she had treated her in return.

But maybe now that their social circles had collided, Victoria could make it right. She couldn't change the fact that she had hurt Penny when they were younger, but she could admit that she had been wrong to handle things the way she had. Maybe she could at least mend their friendship.

Her phone buzzing with a call interrupted her thoughts. Her pulse quickened when she saw Mara's name on the screen. "Hey, there. I'm sorry I only have a minute. I've got a meeting."

"I only need a minute, Miss Busy." Mara's bright smile was evident in her voice as she teased Victoria. "But I need a favor. Jenna printed a batch of posters for the fundraiser and I can't get over there to pick them up tonight because I have an early show. Do you think you could represent our committee and do it?"

Victoria couldn't help the grin that spread across her face. "By 'our committee' you mean me and you, right? Our committee of two."

"Hey, you're the second most important member of the committee."

"The second?" Victoria countered, playing along. "And you're asking me for a favor?"

"Okay, okay," Mara backtracked with a laugh. "You are the most important member of the committee. So, please, can you do it?"

"Yeah, I can do it. Text me her address and I'll stop by after work." She glanced at the wall clock in the nurses' station. "I gotta run. Talk to you later?"

"You got it."

Break over, it was time to get back to work. She headed to the conference room for the weekly meeting with the ER nurses. The charge nurse from the pediatric ward would also be in attendance, expecting an update on Victoria's pet project.

Victoria had thought Maddie, as the PR Director of Emerald Isle Casino, could get some entertainers to visit the pediatric floor. She thought this would be a simple task, but nepotism was doing nothing for her. Even though Maddie was out of the office on vacation, she should still be keeping an eye on her work inbox. Apparently the proposal Victoria had sent regarding the visit was just sitting there unread—or worse—

deleted and totally ignored. Either way Victoria had no update to present at the meeting, so she resigned herself to bluffing her way through it and following up with Maddie later.

She took a seat at the large conference table and dubiously eyed the list of topics written in bright blue marker on the white board. An ambitious agenda for a twenty-minute briefing. Her eyes hit the Pediatric Entertainment line of the list just as Laney, Queen of Hospital Gossip, slid into the chair next to her.

"You. Will. Not. Believe. This." Laney was breathless with the excitement of a juicy scoop. The stethoscope hanging around her neck swung back and forth as if full of pep as well. No doubt she had run straight from her discovery to the conference room to blab.

"Please enlighten me." Victoria leaned back in her chair and crossed her arms, lending only half of her attention to Laney as she watched the rest of the nurses file into the room. Victoria had little interest in gossip about coworkers, but she would get no peace until she allowed Laney to unload her find.

"I just saw Melanie ducking into the supply room down on two with that new vascular surgeon, Dr. Mendez." Laney nodded her head knowingly. "They are totally doing it."

She wasn't entirely sure a nurse collecting supplies with a doctor was evidence of "doing it," although Melanie did have a sketchy reputation for those sorts of things. "I thought Melanie had been hooking up with that physical therapist. Didn't you catch her with him in the Family Conference Room last week?"

"Yep. Literally with his pants down," Laney nodded, a smug, knowing grin fixed firmly on her face. "She is the worst. Seriously. I mean, she must be pretty good at what she does to keep snagging all these guys. But she's the worst!"

Was Laney stalking Melanie or something? How did she know this much about someone else's sex life? Victoria had too much to focus on during her shifts at the hospital to worry about which coworker was fucking which other one—or ones in Melanie's case. Honestly, she preferred it that way. When it came to stuff like that, ignorance was bliss. Luckily, it seemed the charge nurse was ready to get things started. "Katherine's about to speak," she said hoping Laney would take the hint. "We better pay attention."

"Oh god, Katherine." Laney rolled her eyes. "She's so full of hot air I'm surprised she doesn't float away."

In Victoria's experience Katherine had always been tough but fair. She worked hard and expected the same high level of performance from her team. Glad to be relieved from the gossip loop, Victoria focused on the charge nurse as she went through item after item on the agenda.

The meeting went quick enough, and Victoria figured the vague statement she had made about having been in contact with the Emerald Isle about the visit to the pediatric unit had gotten her off the hook, but Katherine managed to pull her aside before she made it out of the conference room.

"Victoria, are you sure your connection at Emerald Isle is going to come through?" Katherine's eyebrows furrowed in concern. "I'm getting heat from Joseph in pediatrics to get something actually on the schedule. If this is too grand maybe we should just go for something simpler. I can make other arrangements."

"No, you don't have to do that." Victoria answered quickly, not wanting Katherine to go down that path. She had said she would head up the project representing their ward, and she would follow through. Her family wasn't big on being there for her personally, but surely when it came to business they would show up. Victoria just had to wrangle in the one weak link in the plan—Maddie. But there was no need to waiver in front of Katherine. "I'll have a date to you in the next couple of days. I just need to lock in the details with Emerald Isle and we're all set."

Katherine's expression relaxed into a smile, seemingly satisfied with the response. "Great. I told Joseph that you're a real star around here and he could count on you." Her tone flattened as she leaned in closer. "Don't make me look bad in front of him."

Victoria kept a pleasant smile in place as Katherine walked away, but the uttered threat gave her a sour feeling in her stomach. After all she had done to separate herself from the family business, here she was counting on them to make her look good at the hospital, the life she had built without them. She should never have let herself get into this position. Now she had no choice but to follow through and that meant playing nice with Maddie.

She blew out a deep breath. *Playing nice with Maddie.* Right. She was going to send a more strongly worded email.

The Vegas afternoon sun glared brightly off the metallic blue hood of Victoria's Subaru as she pulled into the nearly empty lot adjacent to the warehouse-turned-apartment-building where Jenna Cassidy lived. The brick- and metal-sheet-covered building was no treat for the eye, typical of this part of town, far enough from the strip that tourists didn't wander through, but close enough that the contrast from the bright lights and plastic flash of the main drag wasn't lost on her.

Victoria grabbed her oversize purse from the passenger seat and checked her scrubs, making sure there was nothing gross left over from work on her. You never knew after a day in the ER. She had decided to stop at Jenna's on her way home instead of having to go back out later. That way she could spend her evening vegging out on the couch with some good television—maybe a movie—and relax.

Victoria double clicked her key fob, making sure her car was locked as she crossed the lot. Couldn't be too careful. She rounded the corner to the steel door entrance of the building and punched in the code on the plastic keypad to buzz Jenna.

Only a brief moment passed before a voice she presumed was Jenna's came through the tinny speaker. "Come on up."

The bare concrete stairwell was dark and intimidating, with the only light coming from caged bulb fixtures on the wall. Even though she had heard the heavy door slam shut after she entered, Victoria clutched her purse to her side as she climbed the steps to the third floor quickly. Surely all those Pilates classes had given her the strength to make a run for it if needed. To her relief, Jenna was waiting at her unit and ushered her in.

Victoria recognized Jenna as the striking, dark-haired bartender from Game of Flats. "Hi, remember me? I'm Victoria." Of course the women had met at the birthday party, but it had been dark and loud, not to mention it had been Jenna's girlfriend's birthday. There had been a lot going on. Jenna nodded and gave her a friendly smile and she stepped into the large apartment. "Your loft is lovely."

Lovely was an understatement. The large open space was a feast for the eyes. Lit by bright, overhead lighting hanging from the high ceiling, colorful art adorned nearly every inch of the brick interior. One entire wall was a graffiti-style mural depicting an aerial view of the Las Vegas strip. The casinos were cartoonish versions of themselves, including the Emerald Isle Casino, which made Victoria smile. The overall effect was energetic and fun and warmed her with pride in her hometown. Mara sure had some interesting friends.

"Thanks." Jenna looked genuinely pleased at the compliment as she closed the door behind them. Her piercing blue eyes gave Victoria a once over, as if sizing her up, but her smile remained friendly. "The posters are ready. They're just over here."

She followed Jenna across the loft to a corner that functioned as the actual studio portion of the studio apartment. Among the dozen or so canvasses propped up against the wall stood two easels, each holding what appeared to be works in progress. One was a portrait of a woman, the other a night skyline of a city Victoria didn't recognize. Two very different paintings and yet Jenna's touch was evident in both, making something in them seem similar. A large, industrial metal sixties-era desk cluttered with supplies held the stack of posters Victoria had come to collect for the fundraiser.

"So, you're an artist by day?" As soon as she said it, Victoria felt stupid. She was surrounded by Jenna's work. Jenna didn't paint while she was tending bar in the evenings.

"Art is my passion." Jenna's voice was gravely, but her expression was warm as she pushed a hand through the spikey front part of her hair. "My day job is working for a company that does sets for productions at different venues, magic shows, concerts, stage shows, that kind of thing. Mostly at casinos, of course. Bartending at the Flats is what actually pays the bills."

Victoria nodded, familiar with the operations when a new show came to a casino. She had seen plenty of it at the Emerald Isle in her younger years. It seemed as though some of the pieces lining the walls were left over from those productions. Her gaze caught a larger-than-life, gold-framed looking glass that would fit on a stage set of *Alice In Wonderland*. "Did you build that?"

"Yep," Jenna beamed, walking closer to the piece and running her hand along the oversize, gilded frame. "It was a prop from an old magic show they had at the Rothmoor. One of the first jobs I worked when I came to town. The production was just a filler until they had a bigger show take the stage, but I was so damn proud of that set. Penny Rothmoor let me take the piece from their storage room after we met. They weren't going to use it once the show shut down anyway. You met Penny the other night, right?"

Penny. There she was again. And there was that uncomfortable prickle at the base of Victoria's brain as well at the mention of her name. She was going to have to do something about that. "Yeah. We actually went to high school together." At least it seemed as if the entire friend circle had been spared the details of their past. Victoria scrambled to change the subject. "It's so cool that you know how to build stuff like that."

"Like I said, art is a passion of mine. In all its forms." Jenna gathered the posters and smiled again. "Do you need me to help you get these to your car?"

"No, thanks. I can manage." She took the pile from Jenna, tucked it under one arm, and followed her back to the door. Before she headed out, she placed a hand on Jenna's shoulder. "Thanks for doing this. It was good to see you again."

"Happy to help." Jenna gave a nod. "I'm sure I'll see you around."

The stairwell seemed a lot less daunting to Victoria as she headed back down. It felt good to get to know Mara's friends and be accepted into their group. Maybe after the whole dating deal was over, she would even stay in touch with some of them.

It might be nice to have a group of friends like that. Of course, first they would have to get over the fact that she and Mara had deceived them about the whole dating thing.

She hadn't thought that part through, she realized with a sigh. This was never going to be her reality because she was not really dating Mara. She was getting what she needed: someone to accompany her to Grandmother Siobhan's ninetieth birthday, and that was worth the price of missing out on this particular friend set. She searched for a thread of hope to grasp onto. It wasn't a complete lie. They were pretending to date, but Victoria really liked hanging around with Mara. If Mara wasn't such a known playgirl, Victoria would totally date her for real. At least she would if she was considering dating anyone in the first place. So, it wasn't really a lie at all and maybe the group would forgive her.

Victoria had enjoyed the party with Mara. She was funny and good to her friends, and really quite sweet when she was talking about her mother's cooking. That part had surprised Victoria. And the invitation to come over for dinner had surprised her too—along with the rush of excitement that had accompanied it. But Victoria was not getting carried away. It was just a meal with her friend. Nothing to get too excited about or overanalyze. She would enjoy the fake dating for the next couple of weeks, enjoy her new friendship with Mara, and not let any ideas that something could happen between them for real slip into her mind. Victoria would have her date for the party and then life would go on like normal.

Everything was going to be just fine.

Probably.

CHAPTER SIXTEEN

As Victoria rode up to Mara's suite in the elevator clutching a bottle of red wine, her gaze ran along the gold-gilded accents on the paneling of the car. The accents were as extra and ridiculous as the idea of her pretending to be someone's girlfriend. Why the hell had she agreed to this? It was one thing to hang out at a bar with some friends and play the part, but now she was on her way to meet her fake girlfriend's very real mother. Her stomach clenched. This was a task way above her pay grade. All she had wanted was one damn date, not a relationship with a known playgirl.

How did one even pretend to be a girlfriend? She didn't know. She thought she knew how to be a real one back when she was with Allyson, back when she thought she had the perfect girlfriend to attend events, share meals, snuggle on the couch and watch made-for-TV movies. Someone you bought little gifts for just to see the smile that would light up their face. Someone you could confess your darkest secrets and deepest feelings to. Someone you could trust. But since Allyson had walked out on her after three years together with no explanation other than she simply "wasn't ready to settle down," clearly Victoria had been very wrong. She didn't know how to be a girlfriend, real or fake.

The doors slid open and she stepped out of the car. She had arrived but she didn't have to stay. She would knock on the door, explain to Mara why she couldn't stay for dinner, and be on her way. She would still hold up her end of the bargain playing girlfriend in Mara's social circle, but this "meet the mother" thing was way out of the bounds of their agreement.

Halfway down the hall a fleeting thought of making a run for it popped into her head and she turned longingly back at the elevator. As she did, the bottle of wine in her hand clunked against the wall. So much for making a quick and silent get away. She swiped her empty hand over the surface of the wall, praying there was no ding left behind from the bottle.

"Looking for an escape hatch?" Mara, no doubt alerted to Victoria's presence by the knock of the bottle in the hallway, had poked her head out her door. She cocked a curious eyebrow in Victoria's direction.

"No." Victoria's cheeks flushed with heat. Was it that obvious that she was considering a hasty retreat? She held out the wine hoping to cover her embarrassment. "I brought you wine."

"Great!" Mara opened her door a little wider and the delicious scent of garlic and basil wafted out into the hallway. "Come on in."

Victoria recalled a story from her childhood of a little rabbit that famously followed his nose, and for a moment she was certain it was the baking lasagna itself beckoning her inside. She shook her head to clear the vision of bubbling, gooey, cheesy lasagna layers. After all, it was Mara's mother who had created that wonderful smell. How could Victoria go into the suite and scarf down the woman's best dish while lying to her face? "I can't. I'm sorry. I can't stay."

The grin on Mara's face faded. "But the lasagna is almost ready."

Victoria's heart sunk and her stomach growled. She didn't want to disappoint Mara, but she had to stand strong on this. No matter how damn good dinner smelled. "I can't do it."

"Of course you can," Mara encouraged. "Just come in, have a glass of wine and a big plate of heaven."

"I can't lie to your mother."

"You can't—" Mara's face screwed up into confusion while she tried to work it out. "What do you have to lie about?"

Victoria sighed and tears pricked behind her eyes. She hated that she was disappointing Mara by declining the invite. "I can't lie to your mother and say we're in a relationship when we're not. It's one thing to fool your friends, but this is a whole other ball game."

Relief crossed Mara's beautiful features, quickly followed by a bright smile that lit up her face. "Oh, Victoria. I don't want you to pretend anything tonight. That's not why I invited you here. I just wanted to share this with you—as friends. And god knows, we would never fool my mom anyway. I have four older siblings. I never got away with a damn thing. There's no pulling one over on Antoinette Antonini. So, please, come in here. Meet my mom and have dinner with us, as my friend."

The weight of worry that had been crushing Victoria's chest since she stepped into the casino lifted and she returned Mara's smile. The empty space left plenty of room for Victoria's appetite to come roaring back. The smell of baking cheeses and tomato sauce was calling to her by name.

If Victoria had any lingering concerns about meeting Mara's mother, they wafted away like the cloud of garlicy goodness billowing from the kitchen when they were introduced. Antoinette approached her with open arms and gathered her up in a warm, welcoming hug before Victoria could even utter, "Nice to meet you."

"I'm always so happy to meet my Mara's friends." Antoinette released her embrace but chattered away and kept one arm wrapped around Victoria's waist as she ushered her toward the dinner table. The little dining set had been pulled away from the wall in the kitchen nook and the desk chair from the living room had been dragged over to accommodate seating for three.

As Victoria took her place at the table, she tried to remember the last time her own mother had hugged her the way Mara's mother did. Possibly high school graduation? Maybe. Even then it hadn't been the same. Jacqueline McHenry wasn't exactly the touchy-feely type. She was more the keep-people-at-arm's-length-and-air-kiss type.

Antoinette served them each a piping hot plate of lasagna, then passed a basket of warm, crusty bread. As Victoria pulled a slice from the loaf and inhaled the sweet and herby aroma, her mouth watered. "Mrs. Antonini, I've never smelled bread this delicious in my life, and believe me, I'm a big fan of bread."

"First of all, it's Antoinette." The older woman patted Victoria's forearm. "Secondly, I didn't bake that bread, Mara did. And thirdly, if you're a fan, you need to eat more bread. You could stand to put some meat on those bones."

"Ma!" Mara balked.

Victoria shook her head. "Wait. Mara baked this?"

Mara frowned. "Don't look so surprised. I'm more than just a pretty face, you know."

"No, I know that." Victoria's cheeks burned at her foot-in-mouth moment as she took another bite. "It's just…This is amazing."

Victoria savored the light herb flavor before washing it down with wine. She had come to expect some things from Mara—quick wit and over the top jokes, good times and loyal friendship. But baking bread was a surprise. The way Mara gazed at her mother with pure admiration and the way Antoinette beamed back with pride were touching. Victoria envied their mother-daughter dynamic. Yet another thing that surprised her about Mara. The comedian came across as strong, cool and independent. Victoria never would have pegged her as a mama's girl.

"I told you my ma taught me well. Now come on, manga!"

* * *

The women lingered at the dinner table well after the meal was over, drinking wine and talking. As Mara had expected, her mom and Victoria had eased into a comfortable conversation that had a rhythm like they had known each other forever. Antoinette had always been that way with Mara's friends and her siblings' friends. In the Antonini household, once you shared a meal, you were family. It had taken Victoria a bit to settle, but after a little bread and a few bites of lasagna, any awkwardness appeared to be completely forgotten.

Victoria's eyes shone with excitement as she told Antoinette about her latest pet project at the hospital. "I have the connections to bring a little joy to the kids in the pediatric ward. I figured, why not? It's just a matter of pulling the right strings and working my way through the red tape."

"That's a wonderful campaign for you to be heading up," Antoinette said. "Nothing warms the heart like seeing happy children. And I have a feeling you've got what it takes to make it happen. You light a fire under those connections of yours. Don't take no for an answer."

"I don't intend to." Victoria appeared fortified by the affirmation as she took another sip of her wine. Her eyes went wide as she noticed the time on the Felix the Cat wall clock hanging above them. "Oh my gosh, I didn't realize how late it was. I have an early start at the hospital tomorrow."

All three women rose and Antoinette pulled Victoria into another full hug as they said goodbye. "Goodnight, sweetie. It was a pleasure. I'll see you the next time I'm in town. And if you're ever in Miami, you just ring me up. But if you come to Miami, for goodness sake, please convince my dear daughter to come with you. Just tell her it's been far too long since she's been home to visit her dear old mother."

"Okay, Ma." Mara brought the guilt trip portion of the evening to an abrupt halt as she grabbed Victoria's hand and tugged her free of the embrace. "I think she gets the point."

"I'm hoping someone else gets the point too," Antoinette said as she began clearing the wine glasses and dessert dishes from the table.

"The pleasure was all mine, Antoinette," Victoria called over her shoulder as Mara dragged her out of the kitchenette and toward the door. "Thanks again for dinner."

Mara lowered her voice. "She can be a little much, I know." Her gaze ran down to their hands, still clasped together. The soft touch seemed natural despite their fake couple status. Hell, they hadn't even been pretending to be a couple that evening. So why did it feel so right? One thing was certain—Mara wanted the moment to last, or at the very least, she wasn't ready for it to end. "I'm really glad you came over."

"Thank you for inviting me." Victoria paused in the doorway. Had it been an actual date, Mara would have assumed she was posed for a goodnight kiss. A beat passed with neither woman speaking before Victoria broke the spell. "I'd like to take you out for dinner. Not like a date, of course. Just tit for tat, you know?"

Why did Victoria have to say tit? Mara was having a hard enough time remembering they were not actually a couple and she had to let Victoria walk out the door without thinking about how physically attracted she was to her. Instinctively she released Victoria's hand, creating a little distance between them before the sweat on her palm gave away her true feelings. Victoria had been very clear in her offer that the dinner invitation was not a date. They were just friends pretending to be a couple, and Mara had to shut down any thoughts that they could be more.

Victoria's hopeful expression dropped and sadness flashed in her eyes. It was enough to bring Mara's thoughts back to the present. Mara had left the offer unanswered. Victoria was waiting for her to respond.

"Oh yeah, um…" Mara stammered, reeling in her feelings. Dinner with Victoria would *not* be a date because they were *not* dating, no matter how empty her hand suddenly felt without Victoria's in it. "Dinner would be great. I'd like that."

Mara's cheeks flushed with heat as she silently admonished herself for continuing to think about what else she would like to do—something like take Victoria into her arms, kiss her and convince her to stay the night. She reined in her thoughts and managed to say a proper goodbye as Victoria left, but even after closing the door, Mara still found herself fighting off the fantasies.

It was no use entertaining the thoughts. Mara was truly enjoying the time she was spending with Victoria and sleeping with her would probably destroy that. That was the way it always was for Mara. She was just too ambitious to be a good girlfriend. She would eventually fuck it up. Hell, she probably wasn't even capable of being in love. Nope. Friends was all it could be with Victoria.

Mara rubbed her temples as she rejoined her mother in the kitchen to assist in the cleanup.

"What is it, sweetheart?" Her mother frowned. "And while you're telling me, grab a towel and dry those dishes."

Mara did as she was told, leaning against the counter, settling in with a sigh. "Mom, you know how Gina, Sophie, and Carla always had a million posters of guys on their bedroom walls when we were growing up?"

"Oh, lord, yes." Antoinette laughed and put her soapy hand to her heart. "Your sisters loved a good celebrity crush. They covered their rooms so completely with their posters and magazine pictures, that by the time they graduated and moved out, I'd forgotten what color the paint was on their walls."

"It was like they were able to fall in love so easily." Mara gently placed the freshly dried wine goblets in the cabinet above the coffee maker where they belonged. Focusing on the task was easier than meeting her mother's gaze while she spilled her guts. "But I always felt like I had better things to do than moon over the latest issue of *Tiger Beat*. Did you ever think that I just wasn't able to fall in love?"

"I thought that maybe you had other things on your mind besides going all goo-goo over Justin Timberlake or Nick Lachey. Like maybe going goo-goo over Mandy Moore or Brittany Spears?" Her mother placed a hand on her shoulder and gave her a knowing smile.

"I'm serious, Ma." Mara shook her head. "Did you worry about me?"

"Dear, your sisters were absolutely boy crazy, obsessing over one celebrity after the next. For heaven's sake, Gina dated half the offensive line of the football team by the time she finished high school. Believe me, *that* I worried about. But you…I never worried about you in that way." Antoinette rinsed the last dish and handed it to Mara before turning off the faucet and wringing out the sponge. She sat back down at the kitchen table and pushed the chair next to her out with her foot—an invitation for Mara to join her. "No, you weren't flitting and fickle the way your sisters were. You were solid. I've always known when you fell for someone, you would be sure."

"Really?" Mara slid into the chair next to her mother. No one knew her better than her mom. She wanted to hear more assurances that she wasn't completely romantically challenged. "You always knew?"

"Yes." Her mother patted her knee. "Just like I know something is going on with you and Victoria. Now, are you going to tell me what it is?"

"What? No." Mara scooted back in her seat, startled by her mother's question. She wasn't exactly ready to admit to her part in the dating deal, but she couldn't lie to her mother either. "Victoria and I are just friends."

That was the truth. They hadn't sat too close or held hands under the table. There had been no hugging or excessive touching like when they had hung out with Mara's friends at the club. They hadn't even kissed goodnight. The lonely ache in Mara's nether-region solidly reminded her of that fact. What would give her mother the idea that they were together?

"Just friends," her mother scoffed. "You can't fool your mother. I see things. I saw the way your eyes brightened when Victoria talked about her special project at work and she looked at you the same way when you told her you made that bread."

"Ma, really." Mara shook her head as heat worked its way into her cheeks. "We're not dating."

"Who said anything about dating?" Her mother shrugged her shoulders dramatically as she rose from her chair and kissed Mara on the top of her head. "I'm saying you two have chemistry, but I think deep down you already knew that."

"I just met her," Mara argued. "We barely even know each other."

Antoinette ambled out of the kitchenette, determined in spite of her daughter's protests. "Mmm-hmm. If you say so, dear." She paused before heading into the bedroom. "Listen to your old mother on this one. You've found something special. Don't let her get away."

Mara leaned back in her chair and stretched her legs. Nobody could read her like her mom. Even when she was a kid stealing cookies from the cookie jar or pulling pranks on her older sisters, Mara was never able to get one past her mother. But this was on a whole other level. She and Victoria had gone into the evening purposely not acting like a couple, not wanting to pretend in front of her mother.

She should have been relieved that her mother didn't think she was a hopeless case. Instead Mara was stuck on what her mom had seen between her and Victoria or what her mom *thought* she saw. Antoinette Antonini was rarely wrong, especially when it came to her children, which left Mara with an even stranger proposition as she sat alone in the kitchen with the hum of the refrigerator and the scent of garlic still lingering in the air. Could her mother be right? Was she falling for Victoria?

CHAPTER SEVENTEEN

When Victoria returned home from dinner at Mara's suite, she plopped down on her sofa and wondered what the hell had gone wrong.

The evening had been wonderful all around—the food, the company, the conversation. Antoinette had been an absolute doll, and Victoria had felt welcome and truly part of the family. Antoinette had even said all that stuff about visiting Miami, and though Victoria suspected her true motive was to get her daughter to come home, she still felt the offer was sincere.

Victoria and Mara had agreed they weren't going to pretend to be a couple in front of Antoinette, and once they stopped pretending, it all felt so easy and natural. They really could have been a couple. It was mind blowing. Victoria had been having such a good time and had become so comfortable with Mara that she had actually asked her out to dinner at the end of the night. Of course, she had been so surprised when the words popped out of her mouth that she immediately back pedaled and clarified that it was just as friends. Good thing too, since

Mara had stopped holding her hand as soon as the invite was uttered. Dropped it like a hot cake.

It had been silly for Victoria to think even for a moment that what they were doing was anything more than the set up they had agreed upon. They were fake dating until her grandmother's party and then that would be that. All Victoria had to do was stick to the plan and keep any thoughts that she and Mara could be something for real out of her head. *Easy peasy.* As long as she didn't think too hard on the shiver that had travelled up her spine when Mara held her hand or the jolt she felt in her middle when Mara flashed that big, beautiful smile in response to something she said.

Yep. No problem.

The loud chirping tone startled her out of the trance. She grabbed it from the coffee table and clicked on the call.

"Hi Maddie," she sighed. Not the call Victoria had been hoping for, but it was crazy for her to have even entertained the thought that it would be Mara calling when she had just left her suite.

"Don't sound so thrilled to hear from me." The accompanying little sister eye roll was evident in her tone.

"Sorry," Victoria sighed. "I thought it was going to be someone else calling."

"Still not making me feel any better." Maddie had the pouty voice down pat, even over the phone.

"I mean…" Ugh. To confide in Maddie or not. Always tricky seas to navigate. "I thought it was going to be Mara. I…just got home from her place."

"Scandal! You vixen!"

"See? This is why I tell you nothing." Victoria walked into her bedroom and put her phone on speaker. She tossed it onto her bed so she could multitask.

"What's going on? Tell me. Tell me. Tell me." Maddie was pulling out every annoying sister move in the playbook.

"It's too late for chanting. If I tell you, will you shut up?" Victoria pulled off her top and tossed it into her hamper.

"Yes," Maddie agreed quickly. "So, are you hooking up with Mara even though I warned you about her?"

"Look, you don't even know her."

She was not going to let Maddie get into her head on the subject especially after the way the night had ended with Mara. She still had to hold up her end of the dating deal, though, and that meant convincing Maddie she was really dating Mara. "We met a couple days ago to discuss the Animal Shelter thing that you're supposed to be handling instead of hiding out at some resort and chasing men down the slopes. Sound familiar? We made some decisions on the theme and decorations, and then somehow we ended up…dating."

"You're dating Mara Antonini?" Maddie sounded delighted by this twist. "Hot-cha-cha-cha!"

"Please stop saying that stuff." Victoria dug around in her dresser drawer for her pajamas with the shorts with the cats on them. The memory of Mara letting go of her hand came rushing back, along with the feeling of emptiness that followed that moment. "Hot-cha-cha-cha" definitely did not apply, but she had her end of the bargain to hold up. As far as the world knew, she and Mara were dating. "It wasn't like that. I like her and I think she will make a great date for Grandmother's party."

"You're taking Mara Antonini to Grandmother's party?"

Victoria yanked her pajama top on over her head. "Is there a reason why you continue to use her full name? We both know which Mara I'm talking about. You don't have to specify Antonini." Victoria slipped her feet into her slippers and picked her phone back up.

"I guess it's just because you're bringing an employee of a rival casino to Grandmother's party."

She rubbed at her temples with her free hand. The call was starting to give her a headache. "Look, it's a family party. It's not even an Emerald Isle sponsored event so it doesn't matter where she works. The important thing is I have a date and mother won't try and pimp me out to every Tom or hairy Dick in the ballroom. Mara will make a great date. She's fun and I like her."

"Look, do you like her, like her?" Maddie sounded as exasperated as Victoria felt.

"Yeah, I *like* her like her. I'm gonna ask her to go steady. What is this? Seventh grade?"

Maddie ignored Victoria's snarky attitude. "Then fine. Bring her. I hope your plan works. Do I even get to tell you what I was calling for in the first place? Not everything's about you, Vicki."

How could it be when so plainly everything was about Maddie. "Shoot."

"I was just calling to let you know Gregory has invited me to go along with him to L.A. for the week—he has business there—and I accepted." Maddie's tone had changed back to happy-go-lucky. "So I'm not going to be home for a bit longer."

"What are you saying?" Victoria knew what her sister was saying, but she was going to make her say it anyway.

"I'm saying I need you to cover for me with this thing for Daddy for another week or so." Maddie said the words fast like she could slip their meaning past her sister. "I'm on my way to catch a flight now."

"Another week or so? The fundraiser is in like, three weeks." Not that Victoria wasn't enjoying the time working with Mara and her friends, but she did have her own life to live without managing her sister's schedule on top of it. "Maddie, come on. This is your freaking job. What's Dad going to say when you don't come back for another week?"

"Firstly, Daddy won't even notice I'm not back. He doesn't pay any attention to what I do. You know that. And secondly, if you hadn't been covering for me, you never would've run into Mara again. Now she's your date for the party. So really, it's like you owe me." Only Maddie could twist things around hard enough to make it seem like Victoria owed her. "And since I helped you out with the Mara situation, I'm asking you to help me out. It's what sisters do, Vicki."

Victoria opened her mouth to argue that she highly doubted many people did someone else's job out of sisterly obligation but doing Maddie's job had led her back to Mara. And even though things felt a little weird between them when she left earlier that night, she wasn't ready to throw in the towel. At the very least they could be friends after the party. So she didn't argue with Maddie. Instead she agreed. Like a big old sucker. "Fine, I'll do it. But this time you owe me one. In fact, I need to talk to you about—"

"Giving you the chance to spend more time with the woman you're dating?"

Maddie had cut her off before she could even bring up the pediatric ward entertainment project. Her voice had a laughing lilt to it, full of bravado after getting her way, yet again. "I don't think so. Ciao!"

CHAPTER EIGHTEEN

It was a fact of life that the more Mara needed her hair to cooperate with her as she styled it, the less likely it was to comply. She squinted at her reflection in the bathroom mirror. Her hair was gaining volume by the minute. It was completely out of control. Mara slowly eased the curling iron out of a tangle before slamming it down in disgust on the bathroom vanity countertop. "Why do you hate me?"

"I actually love you very much," Frankie called from the other side of the bedroom where she was digging through the neon green plastic bin that served as Mara's jewelry box. "Otherwise I would allow you to accessorize on your own, all willy-nilly as you do."

"I'm perfectly capable of accessorizing. I just don't like to do it." Mara frowned at her reflection in the mirror and tugged at the collar of her dress shirt. She undid one more button and ran her fingers along the edge of her vest. Frankie had called it dapper. Elegant yet sexy was such a delicate balance. "And I was talking to my curling iron anyway."

"Makes sense." Frankie appeared in the mirror behind Mara and reached over her head to put a necklace in place.

"No, no. No necklace." Mara attempted to wriggle away, but Frankie had her by the neck, shackled by the piece of jewelry. "I was thinking bow tie."

"No bow tie." Frankie shot Mara a stern look in the mirror. She played with Mara's collar, squeezing the fold between her fingertips. "Too cliché. Tonight you're really gonna class it up."

"Fine," Mara muttered in surrender. She didn't have time to argue anyway. She didn't want to be late to pick up Victoria. They were having the "tit for tat" dinner Victoria had invited her to, and Mara didn't want to mess it up.

After Mara's mom left Las Vegas and continued on her way to Aunt Theresa's, Mara had given some thought to their conversation. She chalked her mother's intuition up to an Italian mother's hopeful thoughts for her still-single, thirty-year-old daughter. Yes, Mara wanted to please Victoria, but only because they were friends. They were in this dating deal together, and they might as well enjoy each other's company. As friends. Nothing more.

While Frankie fussed with the clasp of the necklace again, Mara considered the silver chain and black teardrop stone dipping down to her cleavage. It was the perfect complement to the cerulean button down she had picked for the evening. She fingered the faceted stone. "This was in that bin? I think it's Penny's. I borrowed it months ago and never returned it."

Frankie took a step back and looked her friend over from head to toe. "I'm sure she won't mind if you wear it tonight." She grabbed the curling iron and started fixing Mara's hair, running it down section after section in an attempt to tame the madness. "Okay, put on some lip gloss and you're good to go. Where are you taking Victoria to dinner?"

"Actually, she's taking me. We have reservations at Le Table. Eight o'clock." Mara mugged in the mirror. She turned her head, considering her reflection from one angle, then the other. She was pleased. Even with her hair.

"Oh, French. Fancy! What's the occasion?"

"My mom cooked dinner for us the other night, so she wanted to treat me. We've done a lot more staying in than going out, and I want to show her I clean up okay." Mara capped her lip balm and shoved it into the front pocket of her pants. That was as close as she was going to come to the lip gloss that Frankie had prescribed. She was a one-and-done girl when it came to make up, but soft lips were a must.

She clicked off the bathroom light and headed out through the living room with Frankie at her heels. "Come on, you got your stuff?" She perched her aviators on top of her head while Frankie gathered her folders and tote bag.

"What is your rush?" Frankie boosted her bag onto her shoulder as Mara ushered her into the hallway to the elevator. "You have almost an hour until your reservation."

"I gotta make a stop. And, now that you mention it, I could use your help." Mara flipped her sunglasses down to shield her eyes from the bright setting sun as they left the casino. Two blocks down the strip was a newsstand with black bins full of flowers that weren't as fresh as she had hoped. At this time of day Mara would have to be a little pickier with her selection, but she would still be able to come up with a beautiful bouquet with Frankie's assistance. That was Frankie's kind of thing: crafty. Yes, Victoria had been quick to point out this wasn't a date when she had invited Mara to dinner, but Mara still wanted to show herself in her most charming light. She wanted Victoria to like her, date or not.

Twenty minutes and fifteen bucks later, Mara's hands were full of colorful blooms and she couldn't have been more proud of her purchase as she rang Victoria's bell. She was still grinning from Frankie's send off—a pat on the top of the cab and sage words, "Go get your woman." Her friends were buying their act as a couple. Her plan was working.

Although it had taken about three steps into the fancy French restaurant Le Table for Mara to know she was out of her element—dress code, giant mirrors in the entrance, snotty maître d'—after five minutes sitting across from Victoria at the table, she found herself surprisingly at ease.

"I love this place. Their French onion soup with the garlic gruyere is to die for." Victoria's eyes sparkled as she spoke. The effect warmed Mara, and she felt the tension in her upper back relax. Victoria's eyes were like the crowning jewels to her outfit for the evening—an elegant pale-pink sheath dress with sexy open-toe heels that made her legs look like they went on forever. "Have you ever eaten here before?"

"No," Mara admitted. Her gaze moved from the delicately detailed mahogany crown-molding to the gold-gilt framed paintings of hunting scenes on the walls. She landed back on Victoria's pink-glossed lips—lips that had a sheen equal to the one on the strand of pearls around her neck. Mara had an incredible urge to kiss her, or at the very least, reach across the table and trace her bottom lip with her fingertip. It wasn't a very friend-like thought, nor was it fancy restaurant decorum, and Mara's sense of good manners prevailed. "I'm glad you like it, though."

"Oh, yeah." Victoria nodded enthusiastically, still all smiles, clearly at home in the elegant surroundings. "At one time I actually knew the sous chef here. He had worked at my father's casino, and…" Her eyes suddenly widened, obviously distracted by something behind Mara that had caught her attention.

Good manners be damned, Mara twisted in her chair to see what it was, but all she noticed was a woman being led through the room by the maître d'. She turned back to Victoria, not understanding her distress. The drained pallor from Victoria's face helped the pieces click into place in her brain. Mara's heart sunk. "Let me guess. That's—"

"Mother." Victoria straightened in her chair as the tall blonde with a smile as fake as her big boobs strode over to their table.

The sudden shift in Victoria's mood couldn't be a good sign. She had gone from delighted enthusiasm to stomach-drop horrified in an instant. Mara steeled herself for a face off.

"Victoria, I certainly didn't expect to see you tonight! I'm having dinner with your father if he ever gets out of that damn meeting and gets here. I've been waiting at the bar forever. Anyway, I'm sure he'll be delighted to see you." Mrs. McHenry fake-gushed as she gave Mara the side-eye-once-over. "And your friend. Isn't she…Well, that's an interesting wardrobe choice for formal dining." The woman's boozy breath seemed to hang in a cloud above the table. Mara suspected she hadn't minded the wait at the bar all that much.

"Mother!" Victoria repeated, this time in a sharp, whispered tone clearly meant to shut her mother up. Mrs. McHenry had already caught the attention of diners around them. She appeared to be the kind of woman who got noticed wherever she went and not necessarily for the right reasons.

The effect of her daughter's distress was lost on Mrs. McHenry who leaned on their table half conspiratorially, half as if maybe she wasn't all that steady on her feet. "Come on. Just because you girls have chosen this lifestyle doesn't mean you have to throw all of society's civilities out the window. Am I right?"

The blood pounded in Mara's ears at the woman's slurred words, but even worse than that was the look of humiliation on Victoria's face which had quickly gone from pale to beet red. Angry tears threatened Victoria's lashes, and Mara wanted so badly to stand and give Mrs. McHenry a piece of her mind. The bitch had gone too far but she knew from dealing with hecklers at the comedy club, arguing with the intoxicated could turn ugly fast, so she held her tongue. The last thing she wanted to do was further embarrass Victoria.

"It was certainly something running into you tonight, Mother. I hope you enjoy your evening." Victoria, still in control of her manners, politely dismissed her mother while keeping her eyes trained on the tablecloth in front of her.

"Oh, well!" Mrs. McHenry raised her voice, further drawing the attention of their fellow diners, many of whom shifted noticeably and uncomfortably in their seats. "I was just trying to offer some friendly advice. Did I say something wrong?"

Victoria sat quietly, still refusing to meet her mother's watery gaze. She looked like she was hoping the floor would open up and swallow her whole. Seeing her like that was the tipping point for Mara.

"Yes, you did." Mara looked Mrs. McHenry squarely in her glassy eyes, unable to stay silent any longer. "And I think both your daughter and I—as well as everyone around us—would appreciate it if you left our table now, ma'am."

"Well, if I'm not wanted…" Mrs. McHenry didn't finish the sentence with words, only exaggerated gestures—one hand circling in the air above her head, the other holding out her glass, wine sloshing over the top with the movement.

"Goodnight, Mother." Victoria shut down the impending pity party. It was clear this wasn't the first time she'd headed off one of her mother's tantrums.

With one last indignant huff, Mrs. McHenry stomped off as best she could while teetering drunkenly in her stilettos.

For a moment, neither Mara nor Victoria spoke. They just sat there, stock-still, waiting for the curious and judgmental gazes of those around them to fall away. When it finally seemed like the casual clanking of silverware and hushed-voiced dinner conversations had resumed as normal, Mara braved it.

"Victoria." She gently took her friend's hand on top of the table. "Are you okay?"

Victoria still didn't look up, but the shake of her head answered the question.

"Do you want to get out of here?" Mara rubbed her thumb across the back of Victoria's hand, trying her best to comfort with the slightest of touches. They didn't need to put on any more of a dinner show. She waited until she saw a nod. "Okay. Go on out front. I'll take care of the check and be out in a minute."

"I don't want you to pay." Victoria looked mortified. "This was supposed to be on me."

"It's just drinks. I've got it. Go."

When Mara caught up to Victoria in front of the restaurant, about half a block from the entrance, Victoria was still breathing heavily. Her chest heaved and she sucked in the still-warm evening air. One hand covered her mouth as if literally holding her emotions inside her. Mara put her hands just above Victoria's hips and pulled her in. "Hey," Mara whispered in her ear. "It's okay."

Victoria shook her head again and closed her eyes. "I can't believe she was there. Of all the freaking dumb luck. My fucking mother shows up on the one night we're trying to have a nice dinner. I hate that I let her get to me. You would think after all these years I'd be practiced enough to brush it off. When she made that comment about our *lifestyle*..."

"Your mom's a b—" Mara caught herself just in time. It was one thing to think a certain way about your own family member, but it was a totally different story when someone outside of the family said something. She tempered her response. "I didn't like the way she spoke to you, and anyway, I think your 'friend' looks quite..." In an attempt to lighten the mood, she searched for that goofy word Frankie had used to describe her style earlier. She raised a smart eyebrow as she said, "Dapper."

Victoria took Mara's hand from her waist and wove their fingers together. "Extremely dapper. And sweet, and...kind. Oh my god. I ruined this whole night. I really wanted to give you an evening that was as special as the meal we shared at your place, and now this. I'm so sorry."

"Not at all." Mara shook her head. Dinner had been a bust, but they didn't need to top it off with tears. She didn't want Victoria to feel worse. "We can still have a nice dinner. Hey, I'll take you anywhere you want."

"At this time of night? It will take forever for us to get a table. Plus, this night was supposed to be my treat and you've already paid for our first failed attempt." Disappointment crossed Victoria's beautiful features for just the briefest moment before she brightened again. Finally, a flicker of her usual self. "Hey, I know a place we can go. It's not fancy, but I can guarantee you a great meal...if you like pizza."

"Victoria, are you kidding me?" Mara grinned back at her, relieved to see her relax. "I love pizza."

As she opened the door to Angelo's, Mara was greeted by a burst of air so thick with garlic and the yeasty scent of baking crust she could taste it. "God, that smell reminds me of home."

"Wait 'til you taste it." Victoria put an arm around Mara's waist and guided her toward the counter. "I know it doesn't look like much, but you're gonna love this."

Angelo's was a hole in the wall, no doubt about it. The space was almost all kitchen. The dining area was crowded with two Formica tables, yellowed with age, and red vinyl-covered metal chairs arranged around them with more than a few gashes that left the spongy cushion inside exposed. A lonely, bare hat rack sat in one corner with someone's abandoned umbrella laying at its feet, and on the opposite wall was a large glass-front cooler housing cans of soda, overpriced bottles of water, and brightly-colored sports drinks. Mara grabbed two cans of ginger ale while Victoria stepped to the counter to place their order. The young, dark-haired guy behind the register, dressed in a white apron smudged with pizza sauce, advised it would be about a twenty-minute wait.

"Come on, let's wait outside," Victoria said, leading Mara back out to a park bench on the sidewalk. They both plopped down with their drinks. She chewed her bottom lip seeming to mull over a thought. "Is that really what home smells like to you? That yummy pizza smell? That's awesome."

"Oh, yeah. My mom is always cooking something. And she's damn good at it too. Well, hell, you know that. No one ever leaves her house hungry."

"Your mom is so great, and I just picture your whole family that way—comfortable, fun, homey. I've never really had that as you may have gathered." Victoria gave a sheepish smile. "I think I'm jealous."

Mara squeezed Victoria's hand, appreciating the compliment. "My family is great. We're close knit and cozy. Even though I've moved away, I still feel that way. But believe me, it's not without its troubles. The closeness has its own price. You're attached and you're tied in. That can be a good or bad thing. It depends."

"I guess it all comes with a price, no matter what." Victoria shrugged. "What you witnessed back there at Le Table—my mom, my reaction—that's the price of my independence from my family."

Mara's heart went out to Victoria. Her mother had been completely crappy to her, hurtful and embarrassing. Mara would have been much more alarmed had Victoria not reacted to the situation. Instead, she had handled it with as much grace and poise as could be expected. Maybe inside she was having a major freak out, but Victoria's outward reaction in the moment had been largely dignified. Mara gave her a lot of credit for that. "I'm sorry your mother treats you that way."

"Eh, it's old news." Victoria shook her head to dismiss it. "But I am curious. What's your price?"

"I don't like to talk about it."

"Of course you don't, but your deep, dark secret is safe with me," Victoria pushed.

Mara tried to fix a smile on her face to lighten things up, blow the subject over. "It's not like that, really. No deep, dark secret. It's just...a family like mine comes with obligations." She flicked repeatedly at the pop tab on the top of her soda can with the tip of her pointer finger, the *thung thung* of the vibrating metal filling the silence. She glanced over at Victoria from under her lashes, hoping to be let off the hook. Nope. She was not. Victoria was looking at her expectantly, eyebrows raised, bottom lip sucked between her teeth, waiting for Mara's response.

Mara hesitated, not used to telling the story. It was something she just didn't share, not even with her circle of friends. But in witnessing the scene with Mrs. McHenry, Mara had been trusted with a glimpse into what made Victoria tick. Trust. That sure felt different and...satisfying. Somehow that made it feel like it was okay to share her own story with Victoria. Mara took a long, deep breath before completely diving in. "When my Dad got sick and things got bad, I was the one who got called home to help. Two of my sisters were pregnant with little ones already running around, the other one was living in Germany— her husband is in the Marines. And my brother...Well, no one ever asks a son to come home like that. So, it was me, the single, childless daughter who was expected to help. At the time I was living in L.A. trying to make a go of stand-up there. I was making progress too, but what could I do? My family needed me, so I went home. I mean, I'm not sorry I spent that time with my Dad. It's never easy to say goodbye, even when you know the end is near, but I'm thankful I got the chance to do it. Most days were bad days. He was sick and tired, quiet and confused. Every once in a while, though, he'd have these moments…and they were so worth it. We would reminisce about family gatherings, or he'd talk about Carla or Gina's kids. The day before he died he had one of those moments and after we exhausted our usual topics, my dad put his hand over mine and said, 'Listen to me, Mara. I have had a rich life with my loving wife and children I adore. I'm a successful man. I know you sacrificed to come home to me, and now my wish for you is to find your own success.'"

"So that's what you've been doing since then—working toward success?" Victoria's voice was soft, as if she understood she had been trusted with something Mara held close.

"Yep. I left the day after the funeral. Except when I got back to L.A., no one wanted me. Someone had taken over my old stand-up gig, and with the way I had just up and left, there wasn't a real chance of getting it back. Luckily I had Penny to hook me up at the Rothmoor." Mara shrugged putting the final piece of her story in place. "I moved to Las Vegas, and I've been working my ass off ever since to make good on my dad's wish."

"That's sweet. I admire how you've gone after what you wanted. And it's nice you have that circle of friends here to support you. I don't have that. It's pretty much just me and Buddy, truth be told, unless you count Laney at work. But we only get along because I don't do anything interesting enough to gossip about." Victoria's expression suddenly brightened. "Ha! Wait until she finds out my girlfriend is the sassy comedian at the Rothmoor!"

Mara gulped hard to keep from spitting out the soda in her mouth. She had carbonation in her nose and watery eyes as she choked the drink down. Victoria had said the word as if she believed their own ruse. Like it was fact. Their situation may have been fake, but there was a strange ring of truth in that moment when Victoria had said the word. Strange, but also…maybe okay? She caught a glimpse of Victoria on the park bench beside her. Here she sat with a beautiful woman who was all dolled up in a designer dress, with her perfect up-do and painted nails, and a blush creeping across her beautiful features. Victoria had been willing to share a pizza with her on a Las Vegas sidewalk if that's what it took to share a meal. That was Mara's kind of woman. It suddenly struck her that she *could* do the girlfriend thing with Victoria. And more than that, she actually wanted to. "Girlfriend, eh?"

"I know it's just pretend…I didn't mean to—"

"Hush." Mara tenderly placed her palm on Victoria's reddening cheek. She locked her gaze on Victoria's green eyes before saying anymore. "Don't you dare take it back. I know. It doesn't exactly feel pretend right now to me either." Her hand slid down Victoria's jaw line before she kissed her, tenderly, right on her perfectly glossed lips.

There it was again, as soon as Victoria tangled her hands in her hair, that tingle beginning in Mara's belly that travelled up to her breasts. It wasn't as if it were the first time Victoria had touched her, but somehow this was different. Mara was filled with head-spinning excitement.

Victoria's tongue traced Mara's bottom lip as she broke the kiss. "I cannot wait to get you back to my place and get out of this dress and—"

"Peperoni and extra cheese?" The dark-haired, sauce-covered pizza guy called out to them from the doorway breaking the spell.

Mara pressed her fingertips to her lips to keep a startled giggle from becoming a full out guffaw, while Victoria waved the kid with the hot pie over and thanked him.

"I guess that thought will have to wait." Mara grinned and scooted back to make room on the bench between them for the pizza box.

"We're only pressing pause. Promise." Victoria raised her eyebrows to emphasize her words while opening the lid, presenting the most delicious-looking pizza Mara had seen since leaving her mother's house. "First, we eat."

CHAPTER NINETEEN

Mara had struggled to keep her hands off Victoria while they downed their pizza, but once they had hopped into the backseat of the taxi, all bets were off. Victoria offered Mara a preview of what she wanted to do back at her place, and the ride flew by as they kissed, touched and teased, not the least bit deterred by the driver stealing occasional peeks in the rearview mirror.

"Are you sure about this?" Mara asked when they had stopped making out long enough for Victoria to unlock the front door of her bungalow. "I mean, I distinctly remember you declaring you were not going to sleep with me when we made the dating deal."

"Let's just say I had a change of heart." Victoria grinned and pulled Mara into her house, shutting the door behind them.

"I like change." She trailed her fingers to the hem of Victoria's silky dress, daring to curl them under the edge and brush against skin. Victoria sighed and the sound of her pleasure caused heat to slide from Mara's core downward, pulsing between her legs. With one fluid move, she pulled Victoria's dress over her head and tossed it, along with any other thoughts of the dating deal, to the side.

The contrast of Victoria's coral lace bra against her creamy complexion made Mara's mouth water. She pressed her hungry mouth to Victoria's breasts, inhaling her half citrus-half musky scent.

Victoria's gasp sent another wave of heat through Mara's body and Mara went hard in her bra. Brushing her hand through Mara's hair and tucking it behind her ear, Victoria leaned in and whispered, "Would you like to come in my bedroom?"

The double meaning wasn't lost on Mara as her pounding heart forced a breathy answer past her lips without hesitation. "Yes." She laced her fingers between Victoria's and followed her across the living room.

There was no turning back.

Mara marveled at the change that had occurred between them. This was supposed to be an act. A ruse. Now here they were, unable to hold back the urges drawing them closer and closer. It seemed like it happened in a snap, this change in their feelings. But deep down Mara suspected it was something that had grown the more they got to know each other, as if maybe this was the way it was supposed to happen.

Victoria looked like an angel as tendrils of her sunset-red hair danced across her creamy-skinned shoulders. She reached for Mara, and Mara caved to her request, clutching her hips. Their eyes met, and in that instant, Mara decided there was a connection between them. She needed to know the taste of her and how they felt against each other. She couldn't resist, no matter what the consequences. Her heart wanted to burst out of her chest just from being near Victoria.

She kissed Victoria hard, with a needy, urgent want. When Mara traced her lower lip with her tongue Victoria moaned and a shiver worked down Mara's spine. The misty glow of the streetlamps outside peeked through the edge of the window, casting a romantic light around them, a surreal haze. Mara moved her hands to the buttons of her own shirt.

"Wait." Victoria's voice was a raspy whisper. "I don't want to rush this. Let me look at you."

Victoria's want was so raw, that it sparked a flame in Mara. She wanted it to consume them, burn them up in the heat of desire. This woman was awakening something inside her, something she didn't even realize she'd been missing, something Mara couldn't name in her lust-addled brain, but she didn't want to let go.

Mara took her time undoing each button on her shirt, moving her fingers deliberately from one to the next. She watched Victoria shrug out of her top and trousers. By the time she'd undressed, her body was pulsing with need to make contact with Victoria again.

Goosebumps rose on Mara's naked arms following the trail of Victoria's fingertips. A rush of delicious anticipation flooded Mara and pounded in her ears, ocean waves of lust that could crash over her at any moment. Mara struggled to stand still and let Victoria do as she pleased. She kissed Mara's neck and removed her bra. Her nipples twitched as Victoria took her swelling breasts into her soft hands. As Victoria's kisses trailed across her collar bone, Mara fought the urge to push Victoria onto the bed, letting her set the pace instead. Dominance was usually Mara's thing, but there was something so beautiful and genuine in discovering how their bodies worked together. She couldn't deny the chance for exploration.

As Victoria's lips met the hollow of her neck, a shudder ripped through Mara's core and dampness pooled between her legs. She wouldn't be able to wait much longer. She nipped at Victoria's earlobe, whispering in between tiny bites, "God, Vic, you've got me so wet."

Victoria pinned her against the bedroom wall. Mara had never let it go this far before, giving in to another woman's lead. They could tease, flirt, or test her boundaries, but in the end she wanted to hear them beg for more. And then she wanted to give it to them. But with Victoria she let her guard drop, curious about the sensations stirring inside her, letting the intensity of her need build. Delaying gratification for as long as she could stand it.

"I want this off you," Mara said as she unhooked Victoria's bra and released her breasts, gasping at the contact as they brushed against her own. Victoria drew Mara's bottom lip between her teeth, biting just enough to make her breath hitch and her pussy clench. The urge to top Victoria grew. Mara needed to hear her soft womanly sounds reach a screaming crescendo when she brought her to the brink.

Victoria moaned into her mouth as Mara brought her fingertips to the lacy edge of Victoria's thong. One slow stroke of Mara's fingers across the fabric between Victoria's legs confirmed that she was as ready for it as Mara was. It was time for Mara to take control.

Mara kissed her hard and flipped Victoria so her back was to the wall. Mara was in her element—in control—setting the pace and ready to drive her to the edge of bliss. Taking her wrists in her hand, Mara trapped them above her head and peppered Victoria's neck and chest with more kisses.

Victoria tipped her head back and gasped. "God, that feels good." Her breathing was ragged, her words staccato with the effort of forcing them out.

Mara moaned in agreement. Rarely did an encounter hit her like this, a connection deeper than purely physical. A starting point, not an objective to be crossed off the list. She couldn't remember the last time anyone had made her feel that way.

Dropping to her knees, her mouth even with the thin, matching coral lace covering Victoria's heat, Mara looked up and locked her gaze on Victoria. Things had turned around so quickly for them. Could it really have been only a week ago that Victoria had stated so adamantly that she wasn't going to sleep with Mara? "Are you still okay with this? Do you want me to stop?"

"Absolutely not." Victoria tangled Mara's hair in her hands and pulled Mara to her, hissing, "Do not stop."

Relief washed over Mara at the lusty thickness of her words. Victoria wanted this too. Desire swelled within her as she breathed in the scent of Victoria's wetness. Mara's pussy lips throbbed in her boxer briefs. She yanked Victoria's thong to her ankles, freeing her from the fabric, and forced her legs apart.

Victoria's toned thighs spread in front of Mara like a beautiful invitation. She couldn't wait any longer to have her.

Mara kissed her way across Victoria's skin and teased her with puffs of warm breath. Each touch of Mara's lips against Victoria's silkiness brought on another flutter of excitement in her own core. With the tip of her tongue Mara worked a feather-light tickle at Victoria's clit before taking one long lick of her sweet, wet slit, opening her to take two fingers inside. Mara pushed in deep and rolled the hard pearl across her tongue.

She moaned and cried, "Yes!" Her hips bucked as her climax built.

She needed to see Victoria come undone, wanted to hear her cry out her name. She drove her fingers into Victoria over and over. Harder. Pushing her closer to the edge. Mara flicked her tongue faster over Victoria's bud, encouraged by the hand tangling desperately in her hair.

"Come for me," Mara begged before drawing Victoria's swollen clit between her lips again.

Victoria's thighs shook and she cried out, tightening around Mara's fingers as she orgasmed hard. Victoria's whole body shuddered and Mara stayed deep inside her, feeling the pulse against her hand.

Mara gazed up at the blissful expression on Victoria's glowing face. It was like she was experiencing every fucking postcoital cliché she'd ever heard, but if the rate of Mara's pulse and the fullness in her chest was any evidence, she was buying into all of them.

As she pulled away to catch her breath, her own heat convulsed. She was so fucking turned on. She slid her fingers out of Victoria's wetness and immediately the absence of Victoria's warmth struck her. She craved it again. Pleasuring Victoria was completely satisfying to her. She needed more of her.

Sweat glistened in the patches of moonlight across them. Mara gave Victoria one last soft kiss on her swollen lips before standing to kiss her mouth. Mara licked her lips, tasting traces of Victoria's juices.

"You taste incredible."

"Mmmm." Victoria smiled against Mara's mouth. "No one has ever made me come that hard. *That* was incredible, Mara."

Mara's breath caught and she swallowed the lump in her throat. The sound of her name on Victoria's lips struck her in a way she hadn't expected. Victoria was still panting from the orgasm, but her tone was clear. She was obviously comfortable with the two of them standing naked and pressed together, saying Mara's name like a habit. As if this was something they had done a million times and would do a million more. Like they had *us* potential. For real.

Mara waited for the urge to run. It always came after she hooked up with someone new—the need to escape before things could get sticky. Before she was trapped in more than she had bargained for, anticipating the surge, ready for her brain to tell her to abort mission, she scanned Victoria's face. Victoria's lips formed a satisfied grin, her eyes still heavy-lidded with lust for Mara. Mara's heart pounded, but the rest of her remained still, tangled safely in Victoria's arms. The usual "get out quick" feeling didn't come.

It suddenly struck Mara—she didn't want to run from her at all.

CHAPTER TWENTY

The buzz of the alarm jolted Victoria awake, and she reluctantly rolled out of Mara's arms to shut it off.

Mara's arms had still been around her. Mara Antonini was still in her bed.

Victoria settled back into her warm spot in the sheets, snuggled next to Mara and smiled. She hadn't taken her guest for a "stay the night" type of girl, not after the warning Maddie had given her. She had fallen asleep, expecting that Mara would most likely slip out at some point before morning. But there Mara was, wrapped up in the sheets and blinking rapidly like her contacts were glued to the inside of her eyelids. She was really kind of adorable all sleepy like that.

"Good morning." Mara's morning voice was raspy and sexy as hell. "I guess I fell asleep."

Victoria considered whether she had enough time for one more round before getting ready for work. The night before had been nothing short of bliss. A repeat performance, even if abbreviated, would be a wonderful way to begin the day. But Victoria had to get to the hospital. She was never late for her shift. She could blame car trouble just this once. Or a sick cat? That was a thing and Buddy wouldn't mind being her cover.

She reached over and brushed a strand of hair away from Mara's face. "We both fell asleep."

"How could we not after all that…last night." Mara grinned and her eyes flashed mischievously, no doubt remembering some of those same steamy moments Victoria's mind had replayed since she woke.

Scooting closer to Mara on the pillow, Victoria kissed her cheek, right next to the soft wisps of hair above her ear. The salty taste of Mara's skin was so inviting, she couldn't resist making contact with it again and again. She trailed her lips down to Mara's neck, eliciting a moan. Heat rushed to Victoria's core, a delicious wave of want, waking all of her. Mara was just so sexy and Victoria wanted more of what they'd shared the night before. It blew her mind how they had ended up in bed. One minute they were eating pizza on a sidewalk, the next making out in the back of a cab, and before she knew it, they were at her house completely tangled up in each other.

Mara turned over, wrapping her arms around Victoria again. Her eyes locked on Victoria's with a spark that sent a shiver down Victoria's bare back. Pressing her lips against Victoria's mouth, Mara played with her hair. Victoria's heat throbbed as Mara's tongue swept into her mouth.

Mara gasped as she pulled away, breaking off the kiss and rolling onto her back. "You are something else and I can't believe you ever declared you were not going to sleep with me while we were fake dating."

That was the most amazing part of all. In spite of all her concerns about sleeping with Mara and getting her heart broken, and in spite of Maddie's warnings that Mara was a total player, Victoria did not regret a thing. Spending the night with Mara felt right and definitely real. It was hard to believe she had denied her true feelings in the first place.

"Well now I know, even if you fake break up with me, it was worth it." She traced the line of Mara's collarbone to her shoulder with a fingertip, teasing her.

Mara scrubbed her hands over her face, so cute and sleepy still. "The thing is I'm not going to fake break up with you."

"I'm glad to hear that." Victoria pecked Mara with a kiss right on her full lips.

A sexy grin slid across Mara's face and she pulled her closer. "I'm serious. I don't want to pretend anymore. I want you to be my for-real girlfriend."

"I thought you would never ask." Victoria melted into the kiss and the soft caress of Mara's arms. A buzz started in her chest and rushed to her knees, then rocketed to her cheeks, a powerful stirring of emotion for this woman who had won her over with her charm, and humor, and heart.

It had been far too long since she had allowed herself to surrender to those feelings—letting her guard down for a woman. She wouldn't have done it for just anyone, but it had been so easy with Mara. So natural. Victoria felt staggering drunk on the rush of pleasure Mara gave her.

Sliding her hand down Mara's curves, she dragged her touch to the folds of Mara's pussy. The silky wetness she found caused her pulse to race. She continued running her fingers one by one across the ridge of Mara's pulsating lips. "You know, maybe we should fuck again just to make sure."

Mara laughed breathily, tickling Victoria's neck. "I wouldn't mind that one bit, but I know you have to get to work, and I'd hate to be responsible for holding you back."

"I've got plenty of time," Victoria lied, unconvincingly.

Mara slid Victoria's hand between her legs and then pulled it up to her mouth, lightly kissing her knuckles. One of Mara's wild curls fell across her face and her brown eyes sparkled with golden flecks of mirth. "As much as I want to—and I really, really want to—I think we need to take a raincheck on this and preserve your nursely integrity."

Victoria couldn't hold in a laugh. "My nursely integrity? Really?"

"Yes. You need to get ready for work and I'm not going to take the blame for you being late. But we will continue this later. I promise that." Mara gave a wink. "Now that we're together for real, we have all the time in the world. Hit the showers."

Victoria groaned and slipped out of bed. Mara rolled onto her side, making an unexpected sweet, sleepy noise. She had thought Mara was too cool to make cute sounds, even when half-asleep. But there she was, in Victoria's bed, sighing peacefully and drifting back into slumber. It was still a bit of a shock. There were a lot of things Victoria was finding herself rethinking. And things were only getting better as she did. She smiled as she got ready for work and left her girlfriend in her bed to sleep. Mara was right. They had all the time in the world.

CHAPTER TWENTY-ONE

Victoria stood in her living room giving the movie-crammed DVD towers against the wall a critical once over. Earlier in the day she had noticed a couple of the discs seemed out of alphabetical order and it had been bugging her ever since. Scanning the titles, she found *50 First Dates* completely out of place. That one was a little tricky since it started with a number. She plucked it from the rack and placed it back into proper position. She briefly considered rearranging all of the discs by spine color. That might be more pleasing to the eye. Such a big project, though, and she didn't have the time at the moment. Alphabetical was the way to go. It made more sense anyway. One last switch—*Scrooged* and *Scooby Doo* (Sarah Michelle Gellar!). Everything was back in its rightful place. Stress tidying, plain and simple. But if that was what it took to keep her anxiety in check, so be it. There were way worse habits she could indulge in. At least this one was productive.

The anxiety was a result of Victoria's upcoming meeting at Café Gato. It would be her first time hanging out with Mara's friends since the two of them had become an actual, real couple.

Sure, they had mixed and mingled socially before, but that was scenes from a play to Victoria. She had been acting a part—none of it was real. This was a whole different ballgame. She was Mara's girlfriend, and these were Mara's friends. Before she didn't really care what they thought of her. Suddenly, she did. Funny how perspective worked.

"I can do this, Buddy." Victoria reached down to pet the cat as he twisted between her ankles, rubbing against her legs in his spry, cat way.

She double checked her tote of materials for the meeting—invoices for the decorations she had already ordered, notebook for planning, different colored pens in case anything needed color-coding. She was set. She just needed to grab her purse when Mara picked her up and she would be ready to walk out the door.

Victoria was grabbing a water bottle from the fridge when she heard the doorbell. She glanced at the clock. Mara wasn't supposed to arrive for another fifteen minutes and it wasn't like her to be early.

"Coming!" she called as the bell chimed a second time while she was on route to the front of the house. She could see through the skinny glass window that flanked the door jamb that it wasn't Mara.

It was her sister, Maddie.

"Surprise—I'm back!" Maddie pushed past Victoria, walking in like she owned the place. "You are officially off the hook for this animal fundraiser thingy."

"What do you mean off the hook?" Victoria followed her sister into the kitchen where Maddie helped herself to a Vitamin Water from the fridge like she owned the freaking place.

Maddie took a long swig from the bottle, no doubt still down fluids from her extended skiing, drinking, sex-filled trip. "You don't have to go to any more of these fundraiser planning sessions. I know you hate them. I'll take it from here, just like I promised, see?"

Not exactly like she promised. Maddie was supposed to have been back in town a week before. Then she had run off with some guy without even giving an actual return date. Victoria chewed the nail on her pinky finger, debating whether or not to point out this inconsistency to her sister. Victoria had kept up her part of the bargain, helping to plan the event and then actually helping to pull it all together. She had enjoyed being involved. She was invested in the animal shelter fundraising event, not just because of Mara. Well, mostly because of Mara.

"But I'm all packed up for today." Victoria gestured toward her loaded tote. "I know what the plan is. The group is expecting me. Why didn't you call or at least text? I didn't even know you were back yet."

"Don't be silly, sis." Maddie rolled her eyes dramatically. "Of course I'm back. I need to get ready for Grandmother's birthday party. It's only a week away. I need a new dress, and shoes, and jewelry. There are a lot of preparations to make. And Greg turned out to be a bore."

Their grandmother's ninetieth birthday party. Wow. Victoria actually had a girlfriend to take to the party instead of a fake date. It was such a weird concept. Mara was her *girlfriend*. She was taking her *girlfriend* to her grandmother's party. She was taking Mara to the party, just as originally planned when they made their agreement, except now they were the real deal. Mara would be a source of support at the party, and no one would feel the need to sic eligible bachelors on Victoria.

"Earth to Vicki." Maddie snapped her fingers at Victoria before uncapping her drink again and taking another hearty swig. "Do you want to give me that tote and I'll take the stuff to the meeting? I'll explain to everyone that I'm taking over for you and you're off the case."

"No," Victoria answered quickly, cutting Maddie off before being completely banished to the no-longer-involved corner. She had come too far to give up that easily. "I mean, now that I've started with the project, I'd like to see it through. You can come too, though. I'm sure we can use all the help we can get. You know how these things are."

"You never want to take part in these things, especially not anything associated with the casino." Maddie narrowed her eyes at Victoria questioningly, then took a quick breath of surprised realization. "This is about Mara Antonini! You're using this as an excuse to hang out with her, aren't you? Oh my god—you're not just dating her, you're sleeping with her! Come on, spill it!"

Fortunately the doorbell rang again, saving Victoria from the high school gossip fest Maddie was attempting to set in motion.

"That's Mara now," Victoria said over her shoulder as she returned to the front door, relieved for the distraction. "And she's not just some girl I'm dating. She's my girlfriend. So act normal and do not embarrass me."

"Me, embarrass you?" Maddie was right at her heels like a little yippy dog as Victoria opened the door. "As if."

"Hi." Mara greeted Victoria with a quick kiss before she registered that the two of them were not alone and took a step back. "Oh, hi. I'm Mara."

Maddie took Mara's outstretched hand to shake it, not at all bothering to hide the fact that she was looking Mara over head to toe. "Maddie McHenry. The little sister."

"Very nice to meet you." Mara smiled politely, but as soon as Maddie turned away, she gave Victoria a what-the-hell raise of her eyebrows.

Before Victoria could whisper an explanation, Maddie continued with her message for the day. "I was just saying that now that I'm back in town, Vicki doesn't have to do the fundraiser stuff anymore. That's really my job, and I'm completely ready to step in for her. She hates this kind of stuff, you know."

Mara stopped in her tracks and tipped her head to the side, regarding Victoria even more questioningly. "You hate the fundraiser?"

"I didn't say that." Victoria's defenses were up immediately. Leave it to Maddie to waltz in after being away for weeks and fuck with the good thing she had going. She couldn't let Mara fall for Maddie's bull. "It's true, I don't usually do things like this, but I fully support the Animal Shelter, and I haven't minded being involved."

"You…haven't minded?" Mara was looking at Victoria like she had grown a second head.

Victoria's gaze moved back and forth between Mara and Maddie tennis-match style before she finally surrendered with a sigh. This was just the kind of chaos that followed Maddie around. She popped in like the wacky neighbor in a sitcom and all hell broke loose. Victoria had to rein it in. "Mara, can I speak with you privately, please?" She grabbed her girlfriend's hand and led her toward the bedroom.

"You two go ahead." Maddie plopped herself down at the kitchen table with her Vitamin Water. "I'll just wait here."

Mara pulled the door closed behind her, shutting them in the room before turning sharply to face Victoria. "Do you not want to be a part of the fundraiser anymore? Because no one is forcing you to do something you don't want to do."

"What?" Victoria didn't like Mara's tone. It felt accusing, as if she was being called out for lying about something. "I never said I didn't want to be a part of Frankie's fundraiser. Maddie and I haven't discussed what has happened since we started planning the event. She just breezed back into town, like five minutes before you got here and started taking over."

Mara stood there, hands on hips, staring at Victoria while she blew out a long breath, as if she was trying to sort out the fact from the fiction. "So you want to stay on board but your sister is trying to force you out?"

"Of course I want to stay on board." Victoria took her hand, relieved at the way Mara's expression softened when they touched. The stress began to melt with the contact. First there was her overwrought anxiety, then her sister shaking things up. She just needed this moment with Mara to rein it all back in. "But Maddie is right. This is her job. I was just filling in for her while she was away."

"That doesn't matter. We have plenty of work to go around, and we all want you to be involved. I want you to be involved." Mara gave a stiff nod like her word was final. Case closed. "Frankie will assign your sister some task and we'll all just keep plugging away."

Victoria's heartbeat slowed and calmness washed over her. Mara had that effect—even when it came to crap from her family. Mara proved that first with Victoria's mother that night, and now with Maddie. "Thanks, babe."

Mara wrapped Victoria in her arms. "Let's get Maddie and get over to the meeting. We can get her up to speed on the way."

The informal meeting was already in full swing when Mara, Maddie and Victoria walked in to Café Gato. It was just Mara's circle of friends gathered around two tables they had pushed together. Victoria recognized Frankie, Jenna, Hayleigh, and of course, Penny.

Penny had the same long, blond hair and stick-straight posture she had back in high school. She was giving her report as they approached. "...and the Luxor, MGM, and Trop, all in to sponsor the event. So I would say, as far as funding for the actual party, we're right on track."

It was funny how one element from Victoria's childhood could trigger so many emotions. Not only had Penny's look not changed from their school days, the familiar voice took her right back to late night telephone calls, swapping secrets and giggling about jokes shared only between the two of them. Victoria could only hope Penny recalled the warm memories from all those years ago as well, and not just the horrible way their friendship had crashed and burned. Penny was important to Mara, and if things were going to be awkward between Penny and her... Well, she didn't want to overthink how that would impact her new relationship.

"That's all I've got for now," Penny continued, rising from her seat. "And I have to get back to the casino. So I'll see you ladies later."

Victoria sucked in a sharp breath. She couldn't believe her luck. She had ramped herself up for a head to head with her old school chum and now Penny was going to slip out and it wasn't going to happen at all. They would have to face the past eventually, but today was not that day.

"Hi." Mara's voice was overly bright and cheerful as Penny spun on her heel and came face to face with the late comers.

Penny's cool gaze traveled down to Mara and Victoria's linked hands. "It's nice to see you again, Victoria." Her words were rushed and her tone was flat, almost disinterested.

"You too," Victoria nodded, ignoring the side-eye look of concern Mara gave her—proof that she hadn't imagined the weird tone in Penny's voice.

Mara turned her attention back to Penny. "Sorry we missed your speech. Wanna hit me with the finer points?"

"The repeat performance will have to wait. I've got to get a handle on…" Penny caught herself midsentence, took a deep breath, and fixed a clearly fake smile on her lips. "I have a meeting with Jerry at the Laffmoor. I really have to go."

Mara and Victoria stood there staring as Penny made a beeline for the door.

"I feel like we missed something more than the finance report." Mara scrunched her face up the same confused way she did when she couldn't make a decision on what beer to order. It was cute when it happened over drinks, but it was weird now. Mara was rarely lost in a social situation. She was always in command. "Do you think I should go after her and make sure she's okay? Do you think she was weird because of us?"

"I think she was in a rush to get to her next destination. She said it was a work thing. I think we should take her at her word." Victoria shrugged, relieved to have the whole Penny confrontation thing behind them for the moment. There was no need to overanalyze and drum up drama where there really was none. "We better sit down. We're so late."

While Mara and Victoria joined the others around the table, Maddie—who had breezed by them as soon as they had walked through the door, missing the Penny situation all together—was already addressing the group. When Maddie finally stopped her, "I just got back into town" monologue, Mara and Victoria said hello to everyone. Frankie waved enthusiastically, Jenna gave a stiff but friendly nod, and Hayleigh smiled sweetly and squeezed Victoria's hand in a semi-shake.

Lesbian circles had to be one of Victoria's least favorite things in the world, right up there with sauerkraut and dental appointments, but the welcoming vibe from Mara's friends was refreshing. Maybe Victoria had been spending too much time holed up with Buddy or buried in work.

While Mara got everyone up to speed on what her committee had been working on, Victoria continued to assess the group. She knew that Jenna and Hayleigh were a couple, but even if she hadn't, Victoria would have known by the way they kept touching each other every two seconds. They were one of those couples. Jenna appeared to be the "show off my girl" type, first putting an arm around her girlfriend, then moving her hand down to rest on Hayleigh's thigh, next leaning over to kiss her on the top of her head. It was nonstop. Hayleigh did not seem to mind in the least. In fact, she seemed to thrive on the attention. Victoria recalled the story about them U-hauling to Vegas after Hayleigh graduated from college. They really did make a cute couple.

Frankie was sitting to the right of Victoria. They hadn't really interacted much since that night in the ER, other than brief hellos and that night jamming out on the dance floor during the birthday party. Now Victoria could see she was one of those zen-minded individuals. Even just listening to details about decoration vendors, Frankie had a serene, yet interested smile. Every so often she would close her eyes and nod in peaceful approval. Victoria expected the word "groovy" to slip from her lips at any moment. The vibrant print patchwork of her tank top looked handmade and the loose-knit shawl she had draped over her shoulders looked as if it could be her own handiwork as well. Maybe she and Frankie would become crafting pals. Victoria could dust off her old paper working materials and get back to that scrapbook of Buddy pictures she had never quite finished…

"Vic?" Mara was waving her hand in front of her face, as if it wasn't the first time she had tried to get her attention.

"Oh, yes! Sorry!" Victoria sat up in her chair and brushed some nonexistent crumbs from her lap like there had been a totally legit reason for her level of distraction.

"Coffee?" Mara raised her eyebrows at her. "Want some? I'm getting myself a cup."

"No thanks, I'm good." Victoria focused her attention back on the group discussion, hoping she hadn't missed anything vital. She would have to review with Mara later.

Maddie was holding court again, handing out her ridiculous glitter-edged business cards while declaring loudly, yet again, that she was the official contact for the Emerald Isle. Where was this dedication to her position when she was on her never-ending vacation with the sorority sisters and boy toys, or when Victoria needed an answer on that entertainment for the pediatric ward? Anyway, it was fine by Victoria if Maddie wanted to take the helm. She was more than happy to work behind the scenes.

Frankie leaned in and bumped shoulders with Victoria, shaking her from her Maddie thoughts. "So how are things going with you two lovebirds?"

"Very well, thank you, although my sister showing up out of the blue really threw a wrench in things." She was pleased by how conspiratorial the conversation felt. It had been quite a while since she had a friend to confide in. Plus sharing secrets put her one step closer to her new fantasy goal of being crafting pals with Frankie. "Mara took it in stride, I think."

Frankie shook her head and the curls poking out from under the yellow bandana bounced and danced around her face. "Mara has a way of doing that. I'm really happy for Mara. And you too, of course! I've been asking Mara forever when she was going to settle down with one girl. We all have. So we're glad that she's finally taken the plunge."

Victoria looked across the table to see both Jenna and Hayleigh bobbing their heads in agreement having heard the exchange. Next to them, Maddie, who moments before had been gathering her belongings to go, settled back into her chair, her interest in the conversation seemed to be completely revived.

Victoria made an attempt to laugh the whole thing off as no big deal. People could change and that was what happened with Mara. "Mara does seem like the life of the party. I guess that comes with the territory of being a comedian." Her flick-of-the-wrist hand wave was supposed to signify the dismissal of the topic.

Unfortunately, Frankie didn't sense that. "Definitely. Back after Mara and I broke up she was especially in Playgirl Extraordinaire mode. Every time she went to the lesbian bar she took a girl home like a party favor. She would say she was too busy to settle down and be serious about anyone. Always focused on her comedy show. I was starting to worry about her, but now she's got you."

"She sure does!" Maddie giggled from across the table, clearly entertained by this revelation. "What a charming story about your girlfriend, sis. Sounds like she's a real ladies gal. She gets around, huh?"

She frowned before looking across the café for her girlfriend. Mara was at the condiment counter doctoring her coffee with sugar and cream. She waggled her fingers in a wave when she caught Victoria staring. Mara had such a beautiful, confident smile. The kind that went from cheeks to eyes and exuded inner-strength and coolness. The kind that fit the title Playgirl Extraordinaire perfectly. She knew Mara's reason for focusing on her career and she respected that, but Maddie's taunt was pulsing uncomfortably at the base of her brain.

"I'm sorry, who are you again?" Frankie asked sharply. She didn't give her a chance to respond. "Mara is one of our people. We can talk shit on her. You cannot."

The childish glee quickly drained from Maddie's perfectly made up face as she grabbed her belongings again. "I wasn't talking…I didn't mean…"

"Of course you did." Jenna's voice was flat, not friendly as she stood up making it clear Maddie was no longer welcome at the table. "Do you need some help getting your stuff out of here?"

Maddie's lips formed a straight line as she hitched her bag on her shoulder. She clutched her notebook to her chest like a protective shield. "No. I'm perfectly fine." She cast one last glance at Victoria who only shrugged her shoulders in response. "I guess I'll be in touch."

"See ya next time," Hayleigh called as Maddie exited the café.

Victoria sunk back in the chair and tried to wrap her brain around the events that had just transpired. Mara's friend circle had stood up to Maddie on her behalf. They welcomed her in and then protected her like one of their own. Her gaze swept around the table looking at each of the women, all of whom had gone right back to their usual conversation. A warmth spread in her chest as she witnessed the way they smiled at one another even as they poked and joked at each other. Suddenly she understood a term she'd heard over and over but never actually experienced herself: found family.

Mara slid back into her chair and set her full coffee mug on the table. "What did I miss?" She grinned at Victoria as she reached down and gave her knee a squeeze.

Even though the true answer was much more complicated, Victoria simply beamed back at her girlfriend and shook her head. "Just the usual, babe."

CHAPTER TWENTY-TWO

Victoria's house was comfortable and sunny the next morning when Mara arrived, and a decidedly all-around better meeting place than the café for discussing fundraiser stuff. Mara toed her shoes off and put her feet up on the coffee table. She made herself comfortable as she reclined on the couch next to her girlfriend. It was just her and Victoria so far, but Maddie would be joining them shortly. They planned to officially hand over all the decorating committee information. If Maddie wanted to take charge, so be it. Mara had enough to worry about—putting together her jokes and script—and it didn't seem to matter that much to Victoria if her sister led the charge. Victoria actually seemed relieved to be taking a more passive role.

"How long before your sister arrives?" Mara leaned close enough to kiss Victoria. Snaking one arm across her flat stomach, she grabbed her hip and pulled her in tight until Victoria straddled her.

"Well, she ain't here yet." Victoria's eyebrow arched as she grinned down at Mara. The ends of her long, red hair brushed Mara's face and neck.

Mara hooked her thumbs through the belt loops of Victoria's low-slung jeans. The pressure of her body against her lap made her crave more contact. Her pussy throbbed, needing Victoria, lusting for skin on skin contact. Mara kissed her, sucking Victoria's intoxicatingly citrus-gloss flavored bottom lip between hers. As she suckled, she gently raked her teeth against Victoria's mouth and tugged at her jeans.

Victoria's hands tickled Mara's arms, resting on either side of her face. She pressed her mouth hard and hungry against Mara's before nibbling her way to an earlobe. "So, I guess it's fine if I do this," she whispered.

Mara squirmed with pleasure and dampness pooled in her boxer briefs. "Don't stop kissing me, baby." She was breathless. "I love the way you feel on me."

Victoria gave a throaty laugh. "Oh, Mara, I intend to do all kinds of things to you that you're going to love."

A shudder ripped through Mara's core, the sweetest kind of anticipation. She flipped Victoria onto the couch, pinning her against the cushions and kissed her again. Her tongue swept into Victoria's mouth to tangle with hers.

They were so caught up in each other they didn't hear the door open. They didn't hear a thing until Maddie slammed it shut behind her.

"Whoa, hey, little sister here. Excuse me! Break it up you two." Maddie marched right up to them, clearly not at all embarrassed to have caught them in an intimate moment.

"God, Maddie, don't you knock? This isn't your house, you know." Victoria wiggled out from under Mara in an attempt to sit up.

Mara rolled off her and crossed her arms. Her heart was still pounding, her hard nipples still aching for Victoria's touch.

Maddie plopped into the floral print armchair across from them, kicking her legs over the side and swinging them like a child. It was no wonder Victoria worried about her so much. Maddie was like an overgrown kid without the innocence. The tattoo of the red heart with a devil's horns and tail on her ankle was a testament to that. "So are you two done getting busy and ready to get down to actual business?" She giggled obnoxiously and inspected her French tip manicure.

Oh lord. Mara was really starting to regret agreeing to this get together. She should have just dropped off the fundraiser information and let Victoria deal with Maddie.

"Speaking of business," Victoria continued, smoothing her hair, putting herself back in order. "By any chance did you look into the Emerald Isle sponsoring a morning of entertainment for the pediatric ward since you've returned from your skiing adventure?"

"It's definitely on my 'to do' list." Maddie had pulled out her smartphone and scrolled down the screen while she answered. Maybe that was where she kept her 'to do' list, or maybe she was not really paying attention to her sister's request. It was hard to be sure, but Mara had a good guess. This girl was not doing anything to win her over.

"Maddie, I asked you to get it on the schedule a month ago and I sent you a reminder while you were gone. Why are you making this such a big deal? I'm putting you guys on the schedule at the hospital for Wednesday morning, the eleventh. Just have the board okay it at your next meeting and call it a day."

"Ugh." Maddie rolled her eyes to confirm she thought Victoria was the stupidest person on earth for thinking it was not a big deal. "That's not at all how these things work. I'll have to get it approved, then I'll have to recruit the talent and arrange the hours with their managers to coordinate schedules and payroll. It's just a lot of…work." It was clear by Maddie's ugly expression that even the word "work" left a foul taste in her mouth, much less the actual doing of any work.

"I'm serious, Maddie. Get it done." Victoria frowned. "I have a lot of people at the hospital counting on me to make this happen."

Mara didn't know the full history behind the conversation, nor was it any of her business in the first place, but she couldn't stand the way Victoria's sister spoke to her. If Mara talked to her sisters like that, she would probably get slapped upside the head. That kind of thing was code in her family. Victoria had been covering for her sister while she played the party girl up and down the west coast, and freaking Maddie couldn't even be bothered to help out with this one task? It was all Mara could do to keep from butting in on the discussion. This was Victoria's battle, not hers. She chewed her bottom lip in an effort not to speak.

"But it would make the kids so happy, and it's great publicity for the Emerald Isle." Victoria argued. "It's a total win-win."

"It's on the list." Maddie firmly dismissed the conversation, her attention fully focused on her phone screen. "I'll keep you posted. So, what about this animal shelter fundraiser thing? Do you have some stuff for me?"

"Yeah." Victoria sighed and stood, her shoulders slumped in defeat.

As she grabbed a white, three-ring binder from the table and explained the different color-coded tabs to Maddie, Mara rolled off the couch and went into the kitchen to get a drink. She needed a break from Maddie, and she couldn't be responsible for her behavior if she had to witness her treating Victoria like crap again.

Mara glanced out the kitchen window overlooking the backyard as she drew a glass of water from the sink. The yard was a shady oasis—the grass neatly trimmed, the flowerbeds lined with cheerful red and bright pink flowers that looked like tiny pom-poms. There was a chance Victoria had hired someone to take care of her yard, but knowing her, Mara would bet she cared for it herself. Victoria was patient, creative, and had a great eye for detail—all qualities that would benefit a garden. The pretty view brought a smile to Mara's face, a smile made all the wider knowing the beauty was the result of her girlfriend's attention and care.

"Babe," Victoria called from the other room, summoning Mara away from her glimpse of serenity and back to Hurricane Maddie. "Is there anything else we need to tell my sister?"

There was something Mara would like to tell Maddie, but she had a feeling "fuck off," wasn't exactly what Victoria had in mind.

"Eh." Mara lazily meandered back into the room. "I think your big, giant binder probably covered it all," she teased. "Oh! Except the jukebox and set. We reserved the job, but the down payment needs to be paid. ASAP. The information is in the binder somewhere."

"Jukebox and set. Info in the binder. Got it." Maddie nodded her head. "No big deal."

"Except it is a big deal because the whole theme hinges on having this set with a jukebox," Victoria said. "Not to mention, we intend to hook it up to the sound system and have it be our actual source of music for the evening. It's vital to the event." Victoria was really working herself up to a steam. It seemed she had finally run out of patience for Maddie just as Mara had. "So, yeah, it's kind of a big deal."

"Okay, okay." Maddie held her palm out in front of her like she was going to break out in a chorus of "Stop, in the Name of Love," a smart-ass smirk on her lips. "Would you feel better about it if I made a note in the binder or something? Maybe create some kind of graph or spreadsheet?"

It was one thing for Mara to tease Victoria about the super-organized binder, but a whole other thing for someone else to do it. When Maddie did it the words sounded much more sinister. Mara literally bit her tongue to keep herself in check.

Victoria stood with her hand planted firmly on her hip, like a mother nagging her children to do their chores but expecting to have to do them herself anyway. Tired, annoyed, and knowing the battle would never truly be won. "Maddie, don't be a bitch."

That was Mara's sign to step in before things really got out of hand. It was time to send little sister on her way. "So, great. I think Maddie has it from here, right?"

Maddie tucked the great planning binder under her arm while she stood ramrod straight, chin in the air, the dignified Head of the Decorating Committee. "I do. There's no need to get ugly, Vicki. After all, you *do* still want me to work out that entertainment for your pediatrics project, right?"

Victoria rolled her eyes as if she was shrugging off the comment and they followed Maddie to the front door. Mara couldn't speak to Victoria's intentions, but she just wanted to be sure Maddie actually left. Mara was prepared to give her a shove past the jamb and slide the bolt if that was what it took. She'd had enough of Victoria's spoiled little sister for one day.

"I'll just let you two get back to what you were doing earlier." Maddie turned back to them just long enough to give an exaggerated, "we're all in on the secret" wink. "I have shopping to do anyway. I need a pair of black Louboutins to go with my dress for Grandmother's party."

"You don't have black Louboutins?" Victoria looked skeptical.

Mara could only imagine what that girl's closet looked like. Probably alphabetized by designer.

"Of course I do," Maddie snapped before bending her voice into a whiny tone. "But not the right black."

Before Mara could ask the obvious question regarding the right black, Victoria grabbed her wrist in a death grip that clearly communicated she should keep her big mouth shut. The longer they talked, the longer Maddie was going to hang around. Instead, Mara smiled, said goodbye and didn't even breathe until the door was safely shut, not tempting fate with further comment.

"My sister, ladies and gentlemen." Victoria threw her hands in the air as if addressing a very large, yet invisible, audience.

"Yeah, she's a real national treasure," Mara agreed, her lips clamped together so as not to allow any harsher words to slip out.

They plopped on the couch and sank into the cushions like they had returned from battle and couldn't go on.

Victoria patted Mara's thigh. "I know she can be a little much. I'm sorry."

"What are you apologizing for? It's her behavior, not yours. Let her own it." Mara tipped her head onto her shoulder. Victoria felt tense and rigid under her touch. The stress of the exchange was evident. "I really don't like the way she treats you. You need to stand up to her. Don't let her get away with it."

"Pffft. That's just her. She and my mother both. I'm used to it. They think they're better than me so they say whatever they want and I just let it go because I know there's no sense in arguing with them. I'll never win."

"Wait." Mara shifted her posture, sitting up and turning to face Victoria. "They think they're better than you, or you think they're better than you?"

"What are you talking about? You've seen the way they act toward me."

"Yeah, I have." Mara nodded slowly. "And I've seen you just take it. You're basically giving them the green light to walk all over you. In my family if someone treats another like crap, they sure as hell hear about it. That doesn't mean we don't disagree on stuff or we never fight. But if someone is acting like a brat, we call them out on it."

"Why bother?" Victoria sat taller in her seat, defensive. Her hand slipped off Mara's leg. "It's not going to change the way they think. It's just going to lead to a fruitless argument and that's exhausting. Believe me, it's better to let them have their say and ignore it."

"But babe, they're not better than you. They have no place treating you that way. You're intelligent and professional. For fuck's sake, you manage that whole group of nurses at work. You would never take that kind of treatment from anyone at the hospital. So why do you think it's okay for your mother and Maddie to do it to you?"

Victoria looked down at her lap as if the wind had been knocked out of her sails. Maybe Mara had gone too far. Maybe she had overstepped. The thought that she had upset Victoria like that made her sick to her stomach and she swallowed down the lump of guilt that was rising in her throat. She knew better than to butt in on other people's family dynamics. She just couldn't stand Victoria thinking she was less than anyone. Mara had said her piece, and that would have to be enough.

CHAPTER TWENTY-THREE

It had been a heck of a day in the ER and walking into her house and immediately being greeted by Buddy rubbing against her legs was heaven to Victoria. It was only a little after four, but she felt like crawling straight into bed for the night. She had a sneaking suspicion it had to do with the stress she was feeling about her grandmother's party. It was wearing her out.

I will be fine… I will be fine.

She would have Mara with her to help her stand tall, no matter what crazy family members might throw her way, and that was a comfort to her. She would have Mara—her actual girlfriend, better than just a date and much, much better than a fake date—with her at the party. She already had her dress picked out, including shoes and jewelry, and even though she was sure it wasn't on Maddie's level of fancy, her outfit was appropriate and she looked damn good in it. Everything would be okay with Mara by her side.

The party was still more than twenty-four hours away, so she had plenty of time to worry about it. Until then, she needed to keep herself distracted and stay in the moment. She and Mara had dinner plans later that evening at seven, which left her just enough time to soak in the tub and let the stress of the workday melt away before she had to get ready.

Buddy followed her through the house as she poured a glass of white wine from the half-empty bottle in the fridge, then headed into the bathroom to fill the tub. She had stripped down to her bra and panties and just taken a swig of pinot grigio, when her phone beeped.

It was a text from Maddie. *I NEED TO TALK.*

Too bad. She was trying to de-stress from the workday. She would have to text her sister back later. Maddie's latest drama of, "wrong shoes for the party tomorrow," or "I don't know which guy to bring as my date," would have to wait.

The tub was filling with water so hot and soothing, even the steam rising from it seemed to have a healing effect. She dumped in some lavender bath salts and felt instantly better at the release of aroma. She grabbed a book from her nightstand to read and make it a proper soak. That was exactly what her tired bones needed.

But before she made it back to the tub, her phone buzzed again. This time it was a call from Maddie instead of text. Obviously her issue was one of pressing concern, at least in her mind. She let it go to voice mail, grabbed a towel from the linen closet and shed her underwear, tossing the lacy thong into the hamper. The ring tone sounded again. Maddie.

But still, something kept niggling at the back of her mind, telling her she should pick up. She could always hang up on her sister if it was something stupid. Her soak would wait a minute or two.

"Hi, Maddie. What's up?" Her words ran together in a rush as she picked up the call.

"I fucked up."

Well, so much for formalities. This was how so many conversations with her sister started; it was hard for her to work up a froth about it. She casually dipped a toe into the steamy water and jerked it right back up when the sting of the heat bit at her foot. She turned the tap to let colder water infuse the mix. Her body longed to be submerged, even though she knew the water was still too hot. Goosebumps rose on her arms with anticipation, and she grew more disgruntled by Maddie interrupting Me Time.

"Fucked what up?" she asked through gritted teeth.

"The jukebox and set builders." Her voice was small, like a guilty child. Victoria could picture her shying away from her as she said it.

Her brain raced trying to fill in the blanks. It didn't make sense. "You forgot about the builders? The one thing we said not to forget? Are you fucking kidding me?" she seethed, half convinced that it was Maddie's idea of a prank. Please let it be a prank. She held back from freaking out in hopes that the punch line would follow shortly.

"I didn't forget about it totally. I remembered it today," she whined. "When I called they said they had booked their time elsewhere."

"But we had them reserved," Victoria insisted. "We just had to make the down payment. You did make the down payment, didn't you?"

"I mean, they left me a couple of voice mails, and I meant to call, but—"

"You didn't call? You didn't call them back?" No. There was no way Maddie didn't do that one simple task. "You didn't make the down payment in time and now we have no jukebox, no set? No builders? Maddie, that's the key to our whole theme!"

"I know," her damn small voice said. "I just fucked up."

"You fucked up? That's what you're going with? This is your job, Maddie. Your literal, actual job. What are we going to do now?" There was no way they could pull off the theme without a jukebox, and there was no way they could hire someone and get the set built with less than one week until the fundraiser. With one action—or lack of action, really—Maddie had ruined the whole event.

"I don't know," Maddie sniffed, her first sign of actual remorse. "Can you help? Do you have any good ideas?"

So typical. Maddie expected Victoria to bail her out again. And Victoria knew exactly what Mara would say—stand up for yourself. But this was bigger than her, bigger than her annoyance with her sister. If she let Maddie struggle and fail, it would impact the whole fundraiser. She had to help. She had to step in and make this right. She couldn't stand by and watch Maddie fail. It wasn't right, not when it would ruin the work of so many of their friends. She could figure it out. She would make everything okay.

"All right," she sighed, her brain still racing. If she made a couple of calls… "I think I can fix it. Meet me at Café Gato in an hour. You're gonna have to pitch in."

"Pitch in on what?" Maddie's tone had taken back its usual eye roll tone.

"Just be there. This is all hands on deck. I'll see you then." Victoria clicked off the phone without waiting for a response. Maddie didn't deserve the chance to respond. Victoria had way too much to coordinate to worry about Maddie's feelings.

I can fix this.

She couldn't do it alone, though. She texted the one person she knew who could build a prop jukebox and a set: Jenna. *Fundraiser 911. Call me.*

Two hours later—all plans of a relaxing soak and romantic dinner surrendered—Victoria found herself in the parking lot behind Café Gato with Mara and her friends attempting to construct a fake juke box.

Jenna had jumped at the opportunity to flex her creative muscles and build a set and luckily she had the evening off from bartending to get a good start on it. She had framed the structure quickly and was tacking on plywood to flesh it out. Hayleigh was assisting Jenna, handing her nails or tools as required. Mara and Victoria stood off to the side following up on the lead Jenna had given them for a DJ. They still needed actual music to go with the fake structure.

Victoria glanced up as Frankie poked her head out of the back door of Café Gato. Frankie was helping out at the café but kept checking up on her friends in between handling orders and keeping customers happy.

"Hey, Penny just called. She said she'll be over as soon as she can. Things are hectic at the casino. There must be something going down. She sounded harried." Frankie shook her head. "I told her we had it under control here, but you know she loves a good project. I think she doesn't want to be left out of the fun."

Right, the fun, Victoria thought. She scribbled a note on an envelope she found in her purse, trying to keep up with the conversation Mara was having on her phone. Teamwork was saving the day. Victoria had been relieved when a few phone calls found everyone so willing to help with the problem her sister had caused but leave it to Frankie to see the bright side in everything and actually label their scrambling as fun.

Mara clicked off the call she had been on and grinned mischievously at Frankie. "I have some exciting news for you. That DJ, Sam, from Game of Flats, just agreed to do the fundraiser."

"Oh, does someone have a crush on Sam?" Jenna stepped back from the completed form of the box, taking a break to admire her work and tease her friend.

Frankie side-eyed Mara with clear annoyance. "I'm sure someone does, but it's not me, despite Mara's twisted fantasy."

"No," Mara argued, "it's the other way around. Last time we were at Flats, Sam was checking Frankie out while we were on the dance floor. I witnessed it with my own eyes."

"Ooooh!" Hayleigh joined in the harassment. "Very nice."

"You people are insane." Frankie waved a hand in the air as she turned back to the café. "That's enough. Everyone back to work."

No sooner had Frankie slipped back into the building than a custom, cherry red BMW pulled into the lot. Maddie had finally decided to grace them with her presence.

"It's about time." Mara grimaced as she watched Maddie slide out of the car on the other side of the lot. "I think I'm gonna run in and grab a cup of coffee."

Mara had made no secret of her feelings of annoyance at Maddie for dropping the ball on this. She had brought it up when they first arrived at the cafe, but it had been a brief discussion.

Victoria didn't want to argue about her sister's behavior—that wasn't going to solve anything—so she just let Mara have her say.

Of course, Mara wasn't pleased that Victoria bailed Maddie out of her mistake either. Mara thought she should have let her sister fix her own mess, but Victoria didn't want to let Frankie down, so she stood by her decision in spite of her girlfriend's disapproval, and hoped a few snarky remarks directed at Maddie would be the end of it.

Maddie sauntered over to Jenna and pulled her Bulgari sunglasses off to admire the artist's work. "Very nice." She flashed her winning, glaringly-bright, overly-whitened, big-toothed smile and put a hand on Jenna's shoulder. "You're amazing."

Needless to say Maddie wasn't exactly winning Hayleigh over. Hayleigh eyed Victoria's sister with a lethal mix of suspicion and disdain.

Victoria stepped in before Maddie could gush anymore or cause any more drama than she already had by forgetting to pay the builders in the first place. "You are just in time for painting. Before we get started, can I talk to you over here for a minute?" Without waiting for an answer, she grabbed Maddie's upper arm and dragged her away from the others. Maddie took tiny, teetering, quick steps in her high heels trying to keep up.

"You certainly seem excited to see me," Maddie said, although her use of sarcasm wasn't scoring her any points.

"Where the hell have you been? You were supposed to be here over an hour ago." Victoria hated how hiss-like her voice sounded, but she couldn't seem to make it stop. She was fed up with her sister's attitude. "The rest of us have been working our asses off to make up for your mistake. You should have been here."

Maddie's eyes narrowed and she shook her arm free of her grasp. "I was at work. I was working and couldn't just dash off on a whim for an arts and crafts 'sesh' with your friends."

"This 'arts and crafts sesh' *is* your job. Do you not get that?" Victoria couldn't help noticing Maddie had arrived wearing a pale-pink knit sleeveless top, True Religion cropped jeans and

Kate Spade heels, not exactly building and painting clothes. She clearly had no intention of pitching in. Victoria doubted she even knew what pitching in meant.

"It looks like you have everything under control anyway. I knew you could do it." Maddie softened her tone and tipped her head to the side, sweet and innocent.

The manipulation attempt was not working on Victoria. "Maddie, do you have any idea…"

The back door of the café swung open and Victoria turned to see Mara coming back with Penny in tow.

"Look what the cat dragged in!"

Hayleigh ran over to hug Penny. "Hey girl!"

Everyone else seemed to actually be having a good time while Victoria was fuming about her damn sister's bratty attitude. She didn't want to fight about what Maddie didn't do and what she should have done, especially when she knew damn well it would be a fruitless exercise. She turned back to Maddie. "You're right. I do have this under control. So you can go. Go back to your work or whatever the hell you do at the casino. We've got this."

Before Maddie could respond, Penny approached the sisters, her brows furrowed and concerned frown on her lips. "Hey, I'm sorry I'm late. We've got a real situation at the Rothmoor."

"No worries." Victoria shook her head. There was still a slight haze of weirdness in the air as she interacted with Penny again as if nothing ever happened between them. Completely ignoring the past. It suddenly felt uneasy and uncomfortable and…

"Awkward!" Maddie's gaze went back and forth between Penny and Victoria so fast it was like she was observing an Olympic ping-pong match. Her penciled eyebrows were raised, accentuating her over-the-top eye roll, anticipating sparks to fly or a cat fight, or who-the-hell-knew what. "Well then, I'll leave you two to it."

How could her little sister still be so damn embarrassing as an adult. "Bye, Maddie," Victoria waved.

Penny waited for Maddie to saunter off before turning back to Victoria. "Um, is this awkward?"

"No." Who was she kidding? She sighed. "Yes. I mean, I don't know. Shouldn't it be?"

"It doesn't have to be." Penny's tone was clipped and business like—exactly what Victoria expected from her.

She didn't want things to be cold and formal, not if she and Mara were going to be a couple. She had to at least let Penny know she regretted her past actions. That she wasn't the same scared little girl she was then. "I…owe you an apology. It's long overdue."

"You don't owe me anything."

"I do. I…" There was no good excuse for her behavior when they were in school. She owed Penny honesty. "I'm sorry. I was a kid. You awakened these feelings in me that I didn't know I could have. I was…confused. Scared. The way I dealt with it was wrong. I hurt you and I never meant to do that. If I broke your heart, please know that mine broke that night too. You were so confident and sure of yourself, and I was just…scared. It took me a long time to be comfortable with who I am."

Penny stepped closer to her. When she finally spoke again, her voice was softer, kinder, forgiving. "I can understand that. It did hurt me back then. That was the first time I had put myself out there and felt the sting of rejection. It's part of growing up, I guess. More than anything, it was the loss of our friendship that hurt. But I've had time to heal too. Maybe we were both to blame for what happened between us. Or maybe neither of us were." She shook her head and a flicker of a smile played at the corner of her mouth. "It was a long time ago. Either way, I think it's time we let the hurt go."

Victoria was relieved to see genuine peace in Penny's expression, and to finally be able to let go of the guilt that had plagued her since they had bumped into each other again. "So, friends?"

A smile crossed Penny's face and she remembered clearly the heady feeling she had experienced that night in the park so long ago. Maybe they weren't ever meant to be a couple, but there was no doubt they were meant to cross paths in this life. Luckily they would get a second chance at friendship.

"Friends," Penny agreed. "I mean, if you're going to date my best friend, we'll have to be. And since Mara is bringing you around with the group, it looks like you're here for the long haul. She doesn't do that with just anyone."

"Really?" Victoria's insecurity popped out of her mouth before she could stop it. Here she was just reconnecting with Penny and already trusting her with something she had been afraid to even say out loud. Hot embarrassment flushed her cheeks. She breathed out a surrendering sigh. "Everyone's always talking about Mara's reputation with the ladies, and I don't know what would make me so special that I could actually hold on to her. I...don't want my heart to get broken."

"Victoria." Penny put a reassuring hand on her old friend's shoulder. "First of all, there's definitely something special about you. I remember that much from high school. I'm certain Mara knows that too. And I've been friends with Mara for a long time. She's...different with you than she is with other women she's dated. And I swear I mean that in a good way. The best way."

She shook her head with a shallow laugh of relief. "Thank you, Penny. I don't know why I even said that. I need to stop being so scared and have some faith in this relationship. You're a good friend—to Mara and to me."

"Anytime." Penny nodded in the direction of the half-finished jukebox. "Now, let's see what needs to be done here to get this show on the road."

Irrational fears laid aside, she got back to the business at hand. She and Penny walked over to rejoin the others. Despite their little breakthrough, Penny still looked stressed, the smile she was greeting her friends with clearly forced.

Fortunately, Jenna cut right to the chase. "What's up your ass?'

"Ugh." Penny rubbed at her temples, apparently relieved to drop the façade. She glanced over at Mara. "Work crap. Ricky Jenkins is talking about leaving the Rothmoor."

"Good for the Rothmoor." Mara snickered. "Ricky Jenkins is an ass."

"Yeah, that's true." Penny shook her head sadly. "But him quitting with almost no notice doesn't make my day any easier."

CHAPTER TWENTY-FOUR

Mara stood in front of the mirror in the super elegant ladies' parlor at the Emerald Isle Casino and checked her reflection one last time before heading back to the ballroom. Seriously, the giant bathroom had more red velvet upholstered furniture than a whorehouse. Fancy schmancy. She had arrived at the party venue early to be by Vic's side when the first guests arrived, but she'd taken this quick break to freshen up and catch her breath. Her hair was a little poofier than usual, but that always happened when she was nervous. Truth be told, she was feeling a little uneasy about another run in with Mrs. McHenry. The last time they had met, Mara had struggled to keep her emotions in check and not tell the woman off. How would she handle it if Mrs. McHenry started in on Victoria again? Victoria would never forgive Mara if she made a scene at her grandmother's ninetieth birthday party, but she couldn't stand by while Mrs. McHenry steamrolled Victoria like she had at the restaurant that night.

The wheels were spinning in Mara's head—Victoria could practically see them. If the headliner at the Laffmoor left, what would that mean for her girlfriend? This could be the break Mara had been waiting for.

Penny clearly didn't share Mara's hopefulness at this turn of events at the Rothmoor. To Penny, this was a major problem. Losing a headliner unexpectedly was not a good thing for a casino. Victoria might have stayed out of the family business as an adult, but she had been exposed to it long enough to know a few things about how it worked. A change like this was a big deal, and the possibility of losing the headliner clearly had Penny spinning.

"What's going on?" Mara pushed.

"I really can't talk about it right now. I'll let you know as soon as I can. Just be ready—I might need you." Penny flicked her gaze from Mara to Victoria briefly before giving her best friend a more meaningful look. "The Rothmoor might need you."

Mara mockingly grabbed at her chest with a chuckle. "Ready? I was born ready!"

She pushed her hands through the curls trying to tame them, just as she was trying to get her thoughts under control, but each stroke only seemed to make her hair bigger. *Oh, fuck it.*

She needed to get back to the celebration.

The sparkling chandeliers cast an elegant light on the crowd in the ballroom as guests mixed and mingled and wished Victoria's grandmother a happy birthday. The room was full of designer gowns and black ties making polite cocktail hour conversation. The party was off to a great start. Victoria was with her grandmother when Mara entered the room, and they both greeted her with bright smiles as she approached.

"There you are, Mara," Siobhan McHenry, or Grandmother Siobhan as she insisted, said grabbing Mara's arm and anchoring her to her side. "I was just asking Victoria how the two of you met. Sounds like you girls have been up to a bit of mischief lately. But never mind that. I'm just so glad you found each other no matter how it came about."

She should've known Victoria would share the true story with her grandmother. Vic adored her and based on the thirty-or-so minutes she'd known Grandmother Siobhan, Mara could see why. The matriarch of the McHenry clan was the picture of grace with a warm smile that radiated love. Her eyes lit up the moment Victoria had arrived at the party, and the two had been inseparable since. There was no doubt in Mara's mind Vic and Grandma Siobhan shared a special connection.

Mara shook her head at her girlfriend. "Sometimes it's good to preserve the mystery a little."

"Grandmother thought it was funny. She's happy for us." Victoria was gorgeous all the time but dressed to the nines she was completely breathtaking. Her short-sleeve gown had a sequined bodice and a stylish high-low length satin skirt. Her emerald eyes were a striking contrast to the shimmery mocha fabric of the dress.

Mara's cheeks went hot. "I'm not sure what this feeling is but I think I'm embarrassed."

"Nonsense, dear. I got quite a chuckle from the story," Grandmother Siobhan said before turning her attention to a man with salt and pepper hair heading quickly toward the exit. "Robert!"

The man stopped before looking around as if assessing if anyone else had noticed his escape attempt, and then circled back to Grandmother Siobhan.

"Mother," he said in a curt tone. "I hope you enjoy your party. Unfortunately, something came up and I have a meeting I have to attend."

Mother? That was Victoria's—

"Dad, this is my girlfriend, Mara."

Mr. McHenry hadn't been at the party when Mara arrived. She'd seen Vic's mom and sister, but he'd been absent. He must've arrived fashionably late and now he was leaving unfashionably early.

Mara stuck out a hand to shake. "It's nice to meet you, Mr. McHenry."

"Pleasure," he said politely before turning back to his mother. "Now, I really must go."

"It's my ninetieth birthday party. What kind of meeting could be more important than that?"

"Sadly, business calls." He gave a brief apologetic smile before kissing his mother on the cheek. "I wish you a wonderful evening."

As he walked away Grandmother Siobhan tsk-tsked. "Always business before everything with that one," she sighed. "Where did I go wrong with him?"

"Oh, Grandmother, we're going to have a lovely evening," Victoria reassured her. "And maybe he'll come back before the party is over."

Mara's phone vibrated in her pocket, startling her. She'd set it on "do not disturb" mode, so it had to be work. She stepped away to take the call.

"Hey, Jerry. What's up?" She covered her ear with her free hand to block out background noise and focus on her boss.

"Mara. Thank god." He sounded agitated and rushed, not at all his usual smooth as silk self. "Where are you and how soon can you get to the club?"

"I'm…at the Emerald Isle." Mara smiled politely at a couple passing by as she walked out into the hall before responding to Jerry's tone with one equally as urgent. "What the hell is going on?"

"What's going on is Ricky Jenkins is flaking on both shows tonight. His agent got him an audition for some show and he took off for L.A. and now I have no headliner. He was hinting around it all week, but I thought he was bluffing, trying to get us to pay him more. Anyway, I need someone to fill in for him. Can you do it?"

Fill in for the headliner at the Laffmoor for both night shows? Be the headliner at the Rothmoor for two shows? This was just the kind of break Mara's career needed. The thing she had been waiting for since her arrival in Vegas. Her pulse sped up. This was her big break! Except…

"I—" Mara glanced back into the ballroom at Victoria and her Grandmother. Beautiful Victoria ready to celebrate and Mara leaving her to face the night alone. "I have this thing tonight. I don't know."

"A thing?" Jerry was incredulous. "Mara, filling in for Ricky tonight is like an audition. I don't know when Ricky is going to come back, if he ever does. Aren't you the one who said I had to call you first? What about standing up for women in stand up everywhere? Look, I called you first, but if you turn it down, I'll have to work my way down the list. I mean, shit. I'll circle back to you if I need people to fill in later, but if the person who does tonight's shows works out, I might not keep looking."

"Come on, Jerry. I deserve this chance. I've proven myself time and time again at the Rothmoor." It was true. This was her shot to take. She had earned it. Her head tingled with building excitement. She could do this.

"You do deserve it. And I'm handing you the chance right now. Just fucking take it." Jerry blew out a long, tired breath. Exasperated. He was over begging for her. "Mara, I really need a team player here. Can you do it or not?"

Victoria would be disappointed if she left the party, there was no doubt about it, but this was the kind of chance that almost never came along. If someone else filled the headliner slot instead of her, Mara could be stuck in her position at the Laffmoor for a couple more years. She might never get another chance like this—at the Laffmoor or anywhere in Vegas. Victoria would understand.

"Jerry, let me just give me a minute and I'll get right back to you."

"You know what? Forget it, Mara." By the sound of his voice, Jerry had run out of patience for the conversation. "I'll just get someone else."

"No!" Mara couldn't pass the opportunity up. She couldn't let Jerry call someone else. She saw her career, her dreams, her promise to her father, slipping through her fingers. She blew out a deep breath as she made up her mind. "I'll do it. I'll be at the Laffmoor in forty minutes."

"Thirty," Jerry countered.

"Thirty," Mara confirmed.

Ten minutes to explain to Victoria and get to the club. Mara couldn't risk Jerry's reaction if she wasn't on time. For all she knew, he had his next fill-in on speed dial and a stopwatch counting down to her arrival.

Mara had made an appearance at the birthday party as the official girlfriend. Victoria didn't need her there to prove anything. Plus, Victoria was really starting to get a handle on standing up to family members. She had done fine with the Maddie and the jukebox set thing. No, Victoria didn't need Mara now the way she had when they originally made the dating deal. She would be thrilled for Mara and her big break.

* * *

"Your big break?" Victoria struggled to make sense of Mara's frenzied explanation of why she had to leave immediately. "On the same night as Grandmother's ninetieth birthday party? Right now?"

"I know, and I'm sorry." Mara held both of her hands. She'd pulled Victoria out of the ballroom to break the news. "Why don't you come with me?"

She shook her head. "I can't leave Grandmother's party."

"Come on. Besides Grandmother Siobhan, none of your family members have even said two words to us."

"She's the only one who matters." Victoria knew headlining at the Laffmoor was a huge opportunity for Mara, but she wanted her to rush off to the show too? No way. "Grandmother's the only one of them who's been supportive of me since I came out. She's loved me unconditionally. I don't want to leave her on her special night."

"This is a special night for me too, and I'd really like you to be there with me," Mara argued as she checked the time on her phone for the millionth time. "But I can see I'm not going to change your mind, and I'm running out of time. I have to go."

"Then go," Victoria sighed. Out of fight and out of patience. "I've got to get back into the party."

The last bit of hope on Mara's face crumbled, but then her expression turned steely. "Later."

Victoria watched her stalk off toward the exit. Tears of frustration stung at the back of her eyes, but she resolved not to let them fall. She took a deep breath to collect herself. She had to go back into the party and she would be damned before she let anyone see that she was upset that her girlfriend had left. This night was about her Grandmother, not Victoria, not Mara. She would go back to the party, get through the night, and deal with her feelings later. That was it. That was what had to be done.

Scanning the sea of faces in the ballroom, Victoria spotted her sister standing by the bar, and rushed over to catch her before she disappeared back into the crowd. She needed someone who could be a human shield if her mother started presenting potential suitors. "Hey Maddie," she waved.

"God, would you get a load of this crowd?" Maddie's gaze scanned the room while she sipped her vodka and cranberry juice through one of those skinny stirrer straws. "I guess after ninety years of living you collect a lot of friends."

"I'm not surprised by it. Everyone loves Grandmother," Victoria shrugged and ordered a glass of wine.

By the time she'd finished her Chardonnay she'd listened to her sister assess the pros and cons of every single man who dared come into their field of vision and a couple not-so-single ones as well. Mercifully, the staff began to usher the guests into the dining room. Dinner started at eight o'clock sharp.

All through the soup course Victoria did her best to pretend there wasn't an empty seat beside her where Mara should be. She chatted with Grandmother Siobhan, made polite conversation with the others at the table and enjoyed her meal. Unfortunately, when the plate of birthday cake and cup of coffee was placed in front of her an hour later, her act came to an abrupt halt. Her mother, who was on her third glass of wine with dinner, determined the time was right to comment on her eldest daughter's solitude.

"Victoria, did you order a second piece of cake?" Her mother giggled at her own joke, wine sloshing over the rim of the glass she was holding. "Remember dear, a moment on your lips, forever on your hips." This comment was met by a chortle of laughter from both Maddie and Victoria's Aunt Margot.

The wait staff hadn't left any of the other courses at Mara's empty place, but they did deliver a slice of birthday cake. Leave it to her mother to notice something like that since half the time she was completely unaware of anything going on around her.

Maddie and her mother exchanged knowing looks regarding the empty chair beside Victoria. It was more than she could stand. "Don't worry, Mother. Overindulgence is not my problem." She gazed pointedly at the empty wine glass on the table in front of her mother before rising from her seat. She had decided before the evening began that she wouldn't put up with their judgements and rude comments—that she would stand up for herself. If they could throw good manners and decorum out the window, so could she. "Excuse me."

She stood but before she could walk away her mother rose too.

"Where the hell do you think you're going?" her mother hissed, one hand balled in a fist on her sequined-dressed hip, the other waving her wine glass again. "We are hosting a party. You can't just leave your guests."

"I need some air."

"She's upset her girlfriend left in the middle of the party." Maddie shook her head pitifully. "Some girlfriend. I told you something like this would happen with that woman."

Typical Maddie—following in their mother's footsteps. It was so disgusting. Maddie would say anything to remain Mother's little pet, no matter who she hurt along the way, even Victoria. Mara had been right about one thing. She needed to stand up for herself with her family. "I've covered for enough of your no-shows to know how to handle it, Maddie. God knows if I hadn't covered for you yesterday, Emerald Isle would be dealing with some crap publicity about the animal shelter event falling flat."

Maddie's eyes narrowed and her jaw dropped as it registered that her sister had ratted her out. "If you're that put out by me being involved in your projects than you can forget about Emerald Isle sending anyone over to the hospital next week. It's not going to happen."

Victoria's heart jumped into her throat. Even with the armor of anger she had working in her favor, that blow stung. But she'd be damned before she begged Maddie for any favor now.

"Well, I, for one, am glad that woman left," Mrs. McHenry huffed before taking another swig of wine. "There are a ton of available men here I can introduce you to."

"That woman?" Victoria was incredulous. Mara had done nothing but treat Victoria's mother with respect when they met, despite her mother's own poor behavior. Mara didn't deserve to be talked about like that.

"Yes," her mother continued. "What's wrong with you? How could you even think about bringing a woman to your grandmother's birthday party? In front of all my friends? It's embarrassing. I'm only telling you because I care about you. You should know what people would say about you behind your back. It's not pretty."

"Enough!" Grandmother Siobhan took control of the situation. "Jacqueline, you're the only one embarrassing yourself here. The way you're treating Victoria is abhorrent. Now, sit back down, all of you. You're making a scene."

"Mother McHenry, surely you don't think—"

"Hush, Jacqueline." Grandmother Siobhan raised a hand to halt all her blustering. "Victoria, I was avoiding the question knowing you would tell me if you wanted to, but now that the subject has come up anyway, where is your friend?"

Victoria didn't see any reason to lie. "Mara's a comedian and she got the chance to headline at the Rothmoor tonight. She got the call during the cocktail hour. It could be her big break. She had to go."

"Her big break. How wonderful." A delighted smile graced her face and she clapped her hands. "Why aren't you there with her?"

Was her grandmother asking her why she didn't bail on the party? "Grandmother, it's your ninetieth birthday. I couldn't just leave."

"Don't be ridiculous, child. Of course you can. My own son left without thinking twice and that was just for some stuffy old business meeting. This is *love*. This is your girlfriend's big moment. You should be with her."

"Mother McHenry!" Victoria's mother was literally clutching her pearls at Grandmother's use of the word, "girlfriend."

Grandmother ignored her dramatics. "Victoria, go share it with her."

Victoria wasn't sure if it was *love*, she was feeling for Mara, but Grandmother was right about one thing, she should be with her, and if the guest of honor was okay with her leaving, then the matter was settled. She wouldn't waste any more time defending herself or her girlfriend to her family. She was done trying to mend their relationship until her mother was able to meet her halfway. Her mother clearly wasn't there yet, and there was a chance she never would be. Victoria would have to accept that.

"Happy birthday, Grandmother." She turned to look her mother in the eye. "Goodbye, Mother."

CHAPTER TWENTY-FIVE

Mara sat at the bar outside the Laffmoor and took a much-deserved sip of an ice-cold beer. She'd rocked her first set and was pumped to do it all again at the second. It was the absolute greatest feeling in the world. Well, except... She only wished Victoria could've been there too.

She'd been hurt at first when Victoria didn't leave the party with her, but during the cab ride down the strip she had a chance to sort through her feelings. Victoria loved her grandmother so much that it was selfish of Mara to even suggest she blow off her special celebration. If things went as well for the second set as they did for the first, there would be plenty of shows for Victoria to come to. A ninetieth birthday party was a once in a lifetime affair.

Still, she couldn't wait to tell her how fired up the crowd was, how they laughed at her "pussy blocker" joke, how she was in the zone the whole time she was on stage. She couldn't wait to celebrate with her after the night was over.

"They seriously named a bar in this casino the Drinkmoor?" The tall, leggy blonde interrupted Mara's thoughts as she sidled up to the bar and signaled for a drink.

Mara gave the woman a polite smile. "It's kind of a theme they work here at the Rothmoor. Drinkmoor, Laffmoor. You know, Moor is more."

The woman threw her head back and laughed harder than the reply deserved, making her long hair dance around her shoulders like she was in a shampoo commercial. "You are really funny up close and personal too." She put a flirty hand on Mara's forearm. "I loved the show."

See? People loved the show. She was on fire. "Thank you." She raised her beer bottle in a friendly salute before slipping her arm out of her grasp. Time to get backstage and get ready for the next set. She gave the blonde a nod. "Have a good one."

"Wait. Before you go, do you think you could..." She pulled a Sharpie out of her purse and waved it between them.

"Oh, sure," Mara said, taking the marker. She was a rock star. One show as headliner and she was signing autographs in the bar. Wait until Victoria heard this. She reached for a bar napkin. "Who should I make it out to?"

But her enthusiasm deflated a bit as the woman tugged at her V-neck with both hands, exposing way more tit than polite in public.

"I'm ready."

"Congratulations," Jerry said, his timing impeccable as always. He clapped Mara on the back. "You've arrived. Sign the tig ol' bitties and get backstage."

She'd seen plenty of boobs in her day, and these weren't particularly special, so what was with the weird tingling in her scalp? *Oh yeah.* Maybe Jerry felt this was a sign Mara had made it, but she doubted Victoria would see it that way. This might be a part of the night she left out of the recap to her girlfriend. One quick signature and she would leave these tits behind her.

As she put Sharpie to skin, Mara was caught off guard by the blonde ducking her head and kissing her directly on the lips.

"Oh, no!" Mara broke it off, taking a full step away from the woman and leaving a dark slash of Sharpie across her breast. "I'm not..."

Her heart sunk in her chest as she spotted Victoria, still dressed in her beautiful party gown, standing at the far end of the bar. Her hurt expression made it clear that she'd arrived just in time to witness the kiss. As their gazes met, Victoria turned on her heel and strode out of the bar.

"Victoria, wait!" Mara ran after her. "Please."

She caught up to her at the elevators and reached out to touch her shoulder, but Victoria jerked away. To Mara's horror, Victoria's eyes were teary.

"Don't." Victoria took a step back putting more space between them. "Don't touch me. It's just like everybody said. You're a player. And I'm a total idiot."

"Vic, I wouldn't do that to you. It wasn't what it looked like."

"It looked like you were kissing some woman in a bar."

Mara's stomach twisted. Of course that was how it looked, but it wasn't the full story. She needed to explain it to Vic, and as the elevator door slid open, she realized she was running out of time. "I wasn't kissing her. She—"

"I saw you!" Anger hardened Victoria's expression. As she entered the elevator, she held up a flat palm in warning. "Just stop. I don't want to hear it. You're a player, and you'll never change."

Mara had heard the words from her friends dozens of times before, but coming from Victoria, after all they'd shared, it stung. How could Victoria think their relationship meant nothing to her? The hurt made her want to strike back. "I get it. You got what you wanted—a date for the party—and now you don't need me. You can shut yourself back in your little world and lock everyone out again."

Victoria's eyes rounded with disbelief, like she'd been slapped, as the doors closed. Mara was left staring at her sad reflection in the shiny metal. She regretted the words immediately. She didn't want to hurt Victoria. She'd only reacted. Badly. She wanted to be with Victoria. She might even…love her. She'd messed up big time. The clap of a big hand on her shoulder startled her.

"Come on, kid." Jerry's gruff voice was a pinch softer than normal. "You've got a show to do."

CHAPTER TWENTY-SIX

Victoria stood in the dark kitchen and stared blankly at the glass of wine she had poured. The clock on the wall ticked the seconds away. She wasn't sure she wanted the wine. She took a sip and swished it in her mouth before swallowing. She didn't want it. She poured the liquid down the drain. Opening the fridge again, she glanced at the contents. Nothing appealed. She poured another glass of wine.

Fuck.

This was how the past hour of her life had gone. Since she'd returned home from the Rothmoor, nothing was quite right. She couldn't wait to get out of that damn party dress, even though she'd loved it so much when she had put it on earlier that night. She grabbed her most comfy jeans, the ones with the holes down the legs and tattered cuffs, but she realized she didn't want to wear jeans. She changed into pajamas, stepping out of the jeans and leaving them right there in a denim pool on the floor, right next to her discarded bra. She couldn't be bothered with any of it.

She was ignoring the text on her phone from Mara. Actually both of the texts—there were two. She had read them, changed her phone settings to turn the read receipts off and pretended the messages simply didn't exist. She tried to keep up the resistance—to fight temptation—but finally she stopped staring at the second glass of wine sitting on the kitchen countertop and reread them. *I'm sorry. I didn't mean it.* And, *Please, babe, you gotta listen to me.*

She carried her glass of wine into the living room and set it gently on the coffee table before plopping dejectedly onto the couch. She carefully stacked some pillows behind her back. She removed one pillow and threw it across the room. Too much. She didn't need it. She didn't want it. She slammed her palms down on the cushions underneath her and screamed. No words, just a hurt, angry primal scream. Her neighbors would think she'd completely lost her mind if they heard her. Could they have possibly heard? If they did, could she blame it on the cat? *Ugh.* Who cared?

It had been bad enough witnessing that scene in the Drinkmoor, but for Mara to suggest Victoria had only been using her and that what they had between them wasn't real? That had been a whole other knife to the heart.

Buddy poked his head around the corner, eyeing her suspiciously before meowing and slowly slinking over to the couch. He knew she needed him. *Ha.* Even the cat could sense that sort of thing and respond appropriately. Cats were better than girlfriends, really. Mostly. Well, usually. Buddy hopped onto the cushion beside her and curled into a cozy ball. She ran one hand down the soft fur of his back and grabbed the television remote with the other. She clicked through the stations, but nothing caught her interest.

She wasn't sure who she was angrier with—Mara or herself. Every time she thought about walking into the bar and seeing Mara and that woman kissing, she wanted to scream or throw something. Or scream and throw something—hard. Yeah, she was definitely angrier at Mara.

She couldn't believe how stupid she'd been, Mara was a known playgirl, just like Maddie had warned her. Hell, Mara's own friends had warned her. The thing was, when she was with Mara, she didn't seem like a player at all. She was funny, of course, but also so warm and sweet and loyal to her friends. Then there was the way she loved and cared for her family so much. What about that night they'd sat on a bench outside the hole in the wall pizza parlor and shared slices, drank ginger ale from a can, and really opened up to each other? You couldn't fake a connection like they'd shared that night. Tears sprung to Victoria's eyes. Mara couldn't have been playing her. Not the Mara she knew. It just didn't add up.

After ten minutes of sampling every channel offered on her cable package, she settled on a home crafts show on the Go Do It! Network. The gray-haired, apron-clad, welcoming woman had just started poking gold-tipped ivory-colored plumes into a Styrofoam sphere the size of a grapefruit when the doorbell rang. It took Victoria a moment to realize it was actually her doorbell, not the one on the craft show.

It could only be one person at the door unannounced at this time of night: Mara.

She didn't even know what she wanted to say to her. Part of her didn't want to say anything. At the same time, she wanted to scream at Mara and totally tell her off. She really didn't want to fight. Maybe if she just ignored the bell, Mara would think she wasn't home and leave.

The bell sounded again, this time followed by pounding on the door. "Vic, I know you're in there. I'm not leaving until you open this door."

Well, there went that plan.

Despite coming from her big break night at the Laffmoor, Mara sounded miserable and desperate. And determined. It didn't mean she had to open the door.

"Please, Vic, just hear me out. I know what you saw looked bad, but I swear to you, that woman came out of nowhere. She asked for an autograph and the next thing I knew, she grabbed me. And I'm so sorry I said those things. I didn't mean them. Can we just talk this through?"

There was that image again. Some other woman kissing Mara in the bar. Victoria squeezed her eyes shut like she could squish the memory right out of her brain. The last time she was in a relationship, it blew up with no warning. This time there was a giant red flag waving in her face. She couldn't ignore it. She had to shut this down before she got hurt even more.

Mara was still pounding on the door and begging her to listen, but none of it made sense to Victoria. She didn't want to hear what she had to say. There was a reason she shut people out—it was safer. As the tears rolled down her face she clicked off the lights and went to bed.

CHAPTER TWENTY-SEVEN

Tuesday morning Mara sat on Penny's couch, sinking into the plush, overstuffed cushions and wishing they would just swallow her up whole.

Penny was dressed uncharacteristically casual for a weekday in ripped jeans and a threadbare Guns 'n' Roses concert T-shirt. She had claimed she was working on her redecorating project, but the only actual evidence of that was a nearly empty cardboard box on the floor by the fireplace and a red bandana tying Penny's long, blond hair off her face. She brought two cups of coffee from the kitchen and handed one to Mara as she plopped down beside her. "So, still no word from Victoria?"

She shook her head as she blew across the surface of the hot beverage. "No word, no text, no nothing."

She hadn't talked to Victoria since leaving her house Friday night. She'd pounded on that door and begged Victoria to talk to her for nearly an hour, but she got no response. She'd only given up when a neighbor who'd gone outside to let his dog out gave her the hairy eyeball. She figured the cops being called on her would only make Victoria angrier. She tried to text, but Victoria ignored that too.

Mara's stomach soured at the mere thought of how stupid she had been to think she had possibly found real love but still manage to screw it up. Her friends had been right all along. She couldn't handle a relationship. She just wasn't wired that way.

She pressed her fingertips to her lips, unsure whether or not she should admit her true feelings to her friend. When Victoria had refused to answer the door that night, Mara had been crushed. The problem was, she was empty without Victoria in her life. Her stomach was sour, the base of her skull carried a dull, persistent ache, and in spite of the anger that still swelled up in her when she thought about Victoria calling her a player, she had cried more than a few tears over their breakup. Crying over a woman. What had she become? But the tears felt justified. She had been hurt and said things she didn't mean, maybe Victoria had done the same. Still, she wondered if she'd blown the one good thing she'd found in life. Headlining the Laffmoor was good for her career and a dream accomplished, but as far as her heart was concerned, it was doing nothing for her. It was Victoria who brought joy to her heart.

Fine fucking time to realize it.

"I fucked up." Her voice was flat, matching her level of hope that she and Victoria would ever be able to work things out.

"Yes, you did." Penny shifted in her seat, arching her back and stretching her arms above her head, as if limbering up before tough-loving her best friend. "And now it's time for you to stop fucking up."

"She fucked up too," Mara protested.

"I'm sure she did, but if you want to make this work, you have to focus on your part."

She shook her head, covering her face with her hands. Admitting she had been an asshole was much easier than admitting she was hurt. "It's too damn late. It's over. I said… hurtful things that I didn't mean and I fucked it all up." God, she didn't think she had any more tears in her to cry. She was clearly wrong about that too. "Maybe I shouldn't have left the birthday party. Maybe I should have stayed with Victoria. All I could think when Jerry asked me to headline at the Laffmoor was how I was on my way to the big time and how proud my dad would be that I'd finally made it."

"Jerry told me you were his go to gal when Ricky first mentioned the whole audition in L.A. thing, but I never thought he would go to you on the same night as Grandmother McHenry's party." Penny patted Mara's leg. "That was a crappy break, but I don't think the fact that you left the party is really the problem between you and Victoria, and I don't think that means there's something wrong with you. Mara, your career is important to you. There's nothing wrong with that. And there's absolutely nothing wrong with you wanting to make your father proud and wanting to honor him. We all love that about you. God knows that sweetness smooths over a lot of your other crazy, questionable behavior."

"Your point?"

Penny tipped her head and regarded her with a kind smile. "Honey, my point is, your father wasn't famous."

"No, he wasn't. I still don't get it." She dropped her head back against the couch cushions in frustration.

"He wasn't some big businessman or career-before-everything guy. He was a man who valued his family and the people he loved above everything else. Don't you think maybe that's what he meant?" Penny raised her eyebrows at Mara expectantly, waiting for her to catch up. "That he wanted that kind of success for you?"

During that last talk with her dad, he had talked about family and her mom. Looking back on it, no other aspect of life was really mentioned. Certainly not work. Success to her dad wasn't about how far he got in his career, although he had always been a hard-working man. It was all for his family because he loved them and valued them and they brought him joy, just as he brought them joy. Just like Victoria had brought Mara joy. "Oh, my god."

"Yeah." Penny nodded slowly.

"So now I've let down both Victoria and my dad."

"No." Penny took her hand. "That's not what I meant at all. What I meant was, don't let your dad down. Go get Victoria back."

"I can't." Mara was restless as hell. She had failed everyone and there was no good solution. She set her cup on the coffee table and got to her feet. Pacing across the living room floor she turned Penny's words over in her mind. Get Victoria back. Like it was that easy. Like Victoria would even speak to her at this point. "She made it pretty damn clear the other night that she didn't have anything to say to me."

"I'm sure she's had a chance to cool off since that night. It wasn't your fault that woman assaulted you in the Drinkmoor, but think about it from Victoria's perspective. It couldn't have looked good. You can't blame her for being upset in that moment. Then you both said things in the heat of the moment you didn't mean. You made a mistake. You need to make it right."

"I stood outside of her house for an hour that night shouting through the door trying to get her to listen to me."

Penny's forehead wrinkled in concern. "You shouted at her through the door for an hour? And you thought she would like that? I can hardly tell you've never had a girlfriend before," she deadpanned.

"I was desperate. I didn't want to lose her. Plus, I've had a girlfriend," she countered as she crossed her arms defiantly. "What about Frankie?"

"Oh, sure." The worry lines on Penny's face relaxed as she shrugged. "Shall we call Frankie and ask for her input on your girlfriend skills?"

"Point taken." She sighed. At the heart of the matter was that little voice in the back of her mind still murmuring that she just wasn't girlfriend material. She didn't deserve that kind of love. She wasn't capable of it. But if that were true, why did it feel like there was a hole in her heart? Mara had carried around a gnawing pain in the pit of her stomach for the past three days. "Maybe I'm just not cut out for this. I don't think I can be somebody's girlfriend."

"Look, you can do this. You could be the best girlfriend ever. You're just new to it right now. It's an adjustment and you're going to make mistakes, but you have to try. It's just like your career. You didn't give up after you lost momentum when your dad died. You came back and worked like hell to get what you wanted."

"But what if I try and it blows up in my face?"

"What if it does?" Penny forced a laugh. "Will you be any worse off than you are now?"

Mara paused to really consider it. Her heart was already torn to shreds. What did she have to lose? The worst that could happen was that Victoria wouldn't take her back, and that was where she was now anyway. But on the off chance that Victoria did take her back... No, she couldn't entertain that thought. Having hope and then having it ripped out from under you was the kind of shit that hurt. She wouldn't let herself get carried away like that. She would, however, take Penny's advice and try. "Okay. I'll do it."

"That's my girl." Penny grinned, clearly relieved to see Mara behaving normally. "Just be honest with her. Start by apologizing. Admit you were wrong. Do something to make it up to her."

"What the hell can I do to even begin to make up for this mess?" She planted her fists on her hips, spun on her heel and retraced her steps across the hardwood floor. Again. Glancing around Penny's living room, she searched desperately for inspiration. Penny was in the middle of redecorating with Lauren's help, but since Lauren was only in Vegas a few days at a time, the process was slow. The mantle above the fake fireplace was nearly bare, only the weird mime face mask that Penny had owned since college still remained propped up against the wall. Hopefully Lauren's good taste and artistic eye would be the end of that thing. Mara had hated it in their dorm room and she hated it still. It was about two steps away from a creepy clown. Actually, all clowns were creepy in her opinion. When Victoria had talked about having clowns come visit the pediatric floor at the hospital, it had totally given Mara the heebie-jeebies. She didn't know why Victoria wanted... That was it. She faced Penny. "I've got it. I know what I can do but I'm gonna need some help."

Penny stood as if ready to hop into action. "Name it. I'm in."

"Really? You're in?" Mara narrowed her eyes in the direction of her best friend. "You didn't want me to date Victoria in the first place. Now you're going to help me get her back?"

"Mara." Penny sidestepped the coffee table and rested her hands on Mara's shoulders. "Look, when you first started talking about Victoria, I thought she was going to be nothing more than another notch on your bedpost. She and I have history. It's a sordid past in a way, but when we were in high school she meant a lot to me. Our relationship totally imploded, but the truth is, I really cared about her. I didn't want this to be another one-and-done with you. I couldn't watch you do that to her."

"Victoria was never that to me—a 'notch in my bedpost' or whatever," Mara protested, tired of that old reputation following her around, haunting her. "Victoria wasn't like the other women I've gone out with at all. There was something different about her. Actually, there was something different about me when I was with her."

"I know that." Penny placed her palm gently on her cheek, swiping a thumb at a lingering tear. "That's why I changed my mind about the two of you. I could see that something in you had changed. Definitely for the better. I was just too caught up in all the crap going on at the Rothmoor to stop and have a real conversation with you about it. I'm sorry about that. I wasn't a very good friend." She paused and took a breath. "I'm here for you now and you can make things right with her. First, stop talking in the past tense about your relationship. Do you love Victoria or not?"

She eyed Penny like she was a crazy woman. Had she not been following? "I do, but—"

"No 'but.' Tell me your plan and we're going to give it a try. You have to go after her. If you don't, you'll regret it. You have to show her how you feel. Do something. Tell me the plan."

CHAPTER TWENTY-EIGHT

It was the crack of dawn on Wednesday when Victoria passed through the automatic doors of Sunrise General, leaving the already hot morning for the cold air-conditioning of the ER waiting room. Her eight-hour shift was going to begin with the most unpleasant task of telling Katherine, the Charge Nurse, that the entertainment she had scheduled for the pediatric floor that morning would not be making an appearance after all. She should have fessed up to her failure earlier in the week, but she had held out hope that Maddie would reach out and apologize and say the visit was still on. Old habits die hard. She should have known better than to count on her family. That was what got her into this predicament in the first place.

Her shoulders sunk as she crossed the lobby of the ER and her gaze darted to the gathering of plastic chairs where she had first laid eyes on Mara Antonini. Victoria didn't mean to look. She didn't even want to look. It was a habit she had developed over the past month and now it seemed she couldn't shut it off. Every single time she had walked into work since the day she met Mara, her attention had wandered to that spot where Mara had sat in vomit-soaked tennis shoes, cracking bad jokes to cheer up her sick friend. Somehow that woman—the one who hit on her in the emergency room while she was on the job and her friend was puking—had changed something in her.

She wasn't the same timid woman who just took what people gave anymore. She was braver and stronger. She had found it inside her to finally stand up to her mother and speak her mind. She was live-out-loud, why-the-hell-not bolder, all because she had loved Mara.

That last part didn't matter anymore because now Mara was out of her life. Victoria had mulled over in her mind the scene at the Rothmoor a million times. She had been so hurt by Mara that night and blinded by her rage. Looking back on it, she knew she had probably overreacted. Ignoring Mara and just shutting her out like that was one way to make sure they were over and done for good. In the moment it had seemed like what she wanted, but as the days went by she realized she had acted in haste. People made mistakes, and in this case they both had done exactly that. She should have given Mara the benefit of the doubt, and Mara shouldn't have said the things she said. It seemed so simple in hindsight, but Victoria had let her anger and insecurities get the best of her, and now Mara was gone and Victoria's heart was broken.

It was fine, really. She would go back to burying herself in work and eventually the feelings would pass, the hurt would go away. It had to, right? The heart forgives, the heart forgets. Eventually. It would just take time. She had Buddy to snuggle up to on the couch at the end of the day, and he would comfort her while her broken heart healed. The two of them would carry on as they always had.

As soon as she finished stashing her bag in her drawer at the nurses' station, and she broke the news to Katherine about the Emerald Isle visit, she planned on picking up some extra shifts. She could start to claw her way back into Katherine's good graces after the pediatric ward debacle. Hell, maybe she could even stay later after her shift today. It wasn't as if she had anywhere to go. She had planned on attending the fundraiser at Café Gato, but now it was the last place she wanted to land. It wasn't her job, Frankie and Penny weren't her friends, and Mara wasn't her girl. It wasn't her responsibility anymore.

She tucked her bag away in one of the bottom drawers in her desk and quickly typed her log-on into the computer at the far end of the station. Other nurses buzzed around, most of them finishing their shifts. Technically, her shift didn't start for another twenty minutes, but she had left the house early to allow a little extra time for her conversation with Katherine.

"Hey, what are you doing here?" Laney rushed up behind her. "Didn't you get a text?"

"What text?" she asked, confused. She never missed a work text. How could she have missed something? "I didn't get a text."

Laney's eyes went wider at her ignorance. She remained the Queen of Job Gossip who knew everything going on at the hospital, whereas Victoria obviously knew nothing. "You're supposed to be at that meeting in the Family Conference Room in pediatrics."

She closed her eyes and shook her head trying to make sense of it all. "What meeting…"

Laney didn't wait for her response. Grabbing her by the wrist, she dragged her out of the nurses' station to the elevators.

While Laney hummed and inspected her nails on the ride up, Victoria worried. How did she not know there was a meeting? And what was it about anyway? Did they already know the Emerald Isle wasn't sending the entertainment? Did she recall anything weird happening at the hospital lately? Had she been too much in a funk about the whole Mara thing to be on top of her job?

The doors finally slid open, revealing a hallway painted in cheerful primary colors. The Family Conference Room was visible as soon as Victoria stepped out of the car, and through the skinny glass window flanking the door she could see people milling around inside dressed in bright-colored fabrics. She could hear the happy tones of their voices. There was a huge bunch of balloons tied to a chair and a recurring noise that sounded a lot like the barking of a dog. It didn't look like any work meeting she had ever attended.

"Laney, what is this meeting about anyway?" She looked back over her shoulder just in time to get a glimpse of Laney slipping back into the elevator.

"My job was just to get you up here." Laney grinned and shrugged, feigning innocence. She pointed a finger to the other end of the corridor. "Why don't you ask her?"

Coming down the hall from the opposite direction, dressed in a clown costume and holding a bouquet of red roses, was the last person Victoria expected to see in the hospital again.

"Mara?"

There was no mistaking it was her despite the giant clown shoes, white cake makeup, and red nose. For one thing, Mara's springy, auburn curls were piled on top of her head, bouncing in all directions as she moved. But more than that, it was her eyes—Victoria would know them anywhere. It was Mara's eyes Victoria had thought of when she lay in bed at night wondering how the two of them had crashed and burned the way they had. She thought of the golden flecks in Mara's brown eyes, the one that showed in those private moments just for her, when the bravado and showmanship had faded and the real Mara shone through.

That was the woman Victoria met in front of the doors to the Family Conference Room on the pediatrics floor.

"What are you doing here? What is all this?"

"This," Mara tipped her head toward the door, "is a room full of entertainers here to visit the kids in the hospital. And this," she held the bright red bouquet out toward Victoria, "is me saying I'm sorry. I was an ass and I was so wrong. About everything—except that I love you."

Her heartbeat thudded with a strong yearning to collapse into Mara's arms and let the pain of the past few days melt away into a distant memory, except in that moment the hurt was still all too real, and if she ever could shake it, she sure didn't want it back. The fear of that was whispering in her ear, "*Don't chance it. A chance on love is a chance on more pain.*"

The tell-tale prickle of tears played at the corners of her eyes and she struggled not to blink. Blinking would release the tears, and crying wouldn't make any of it easier. "Mara, I can't…"

"Just hear me out." Mara reached out and grabbed Victoria's arm before she could flee. "Please."

Mara's touch still warmed her, even after everything that had happened between them. There was a jolt of excitement and a surge of hope that matched the look she saw in Mara's eyes. She at least owed Mara the moment.

"All this time I've been trying to live up to my dad's words, 'don't give up until you find success.' But I was wrong about what he was saying to me. Success to my dad wasn't about me being famous, or rich, or having the best gig on the strip. He wanted me to find success like he had—a happy home full of laughter and love, a partner to share it with." Mara's voice hitched and she took a deep breath, steadying herself to continue. "I like my job, and I will always want to do my best at work. But you, Victoria…you, I love. And what we had between us—the laughter, the passion, the pure joy in just holding each other's hands and knowing it's the perfect fit—that is success. Definitely the real deal. And what happened at the Drinkmoor, I swear was not me being a player. I was signing an autograph, and that woman took advantage of the situation. I would never, ever do something like that to you. I used to be a player. I'm not anymore. Now I just want to be with you."

A tear slipped down Victoria's cheek, despite her best efforts. Her chest swelled with the emotions she had been trying so hard to fight off for the past few days. The voice of fear was getting smaller and smaller as it tried desperately to cling to her. But what she felt for Mara was stronger. It was time for her to let that fear go and jump in wholeheartedly. "I love you too."

Mara took Victoria in her arms and kissed her, sweet and hot all at once, and right in front of the bunch of gawking clowns and entertainers who had opened the door and were now cheering them on.

Mara broke the kiss and grinned before pressing her forehead to Victoria's. "Guess together we're quite an act. I think we'll have to continue this later. Right now we have a floor full of kids to cheer up."

"But Mara, how did you know Maddie's crew from Emerald Isle wasn't going to show up today?"

Mara grinned sheepishly. "My original plan was just to piggyback my apology on Maddie's group's appearance, but when I reached out to her, she said the whole thing was off because of the things you said to her at your grandmother's party. I knew how badly you wanted this visit to happen, so I called in reinforcements to help out."

"You called in reinforcements to help me even after those things I said to you that night?"

Mara shrugged. "I already told you, I'm in love with you. I'd do anything for you. Even dress up like a clown." She kicked her ridiculous big shoes to emphasize her point. "Now come on. Let's get in there."

They entered the conference room together and Victoria finally got a good look at the cast of characters assembled there—about ten all together. Most dressed as clowns, but there was also a juggler, a magician, a man who appeared to be a strolling minstrel, and three dogs.

"Mara," Victoria gasped as the full concept came together before her eyes. "You really put all this together?"

"Believe me, it was no small feat getting a bunch of Vegas performers out of bed before seven a.m. But I had a ton of help from my friends." Mara winked at Frankie who was dressed as a clown. "And Penny helped too, but she couldn't be here. Plus, she said there was no way in hell she was putting on a clown costume."

That sounded like Penny. Still, all those people at the hospital early in the morning to bring a smile to the children was just incredible, and Victoria was grateful for the effort. "But Mara, you have the fundraiser tonight. And your show today. Don't you have a million things to get ready?"

Mara intertwined their fingers. "That's just my job. This is some important work." She kissed Victoria's cheek before addressing the group. "Who's ready to serve up breakfast with a smile? Let's do this."

There was more applause and hoots of solidarity as everyone gathered their props and dogs and whatever else they needed to spread some joy. Then hand in hand Mara and Victoria led them out into the corridor. At the first shriek of excitement from the little girl in room 402, Victoria knew Mara had been right. This was success and they had found it together.

When Victoria got home after her shift later that day, she was pleased to see Mara was already at the house, as evidenced by the open front door. They had decided to go to the Café Gato together for the fundraiser, and Victoria was hoping they would return to her house together afterward as well.

"Hey, I'm home!" she called out as the screen door sprung shut behind her.

Mara came around the corner from the kitchen wearing a sports bra and boy shorts. A seductive smile crossed her face. "Good, I've been waiting for you. Close the front door."

Victoria did as she was told, but she laughed as she dropped her work bag and approached her half-dressed girlfriend. She had an idea where Mara was going with this. "We have to leave in just over two hours. We don't have time for shenanigans."

"But I'm in the mood for shenanigans." Mara wrapped her arms around Victoria, pulling her into a long, sweet kiss.

Victoria giggled as their lips parted. "I'm sure you are. But there's something I wanted to talk to you about before we go tonight."

Mara leaned back, a look of concern clouding her face. "That sounds serious."

"It is serious." She fished in the pocket of her scrubs pants before pulling something out, hidden in her closed fist. "Mara, I don't want to lose you again and I like coming home to you. So, I'm giving you this."

Mara looked down at her open hand where a single shiny key was offered. "Is that…?"

She nodded. "It's a key to the house. I'm not saying you have to move in now or anything, but I want you to always be able to come here anytime you want because I love when you're here. Because I love you."

"Well I love being here because I love you." Mara grinned mischievously and took the key before pressing their bodies so tightly together their hip bones bumped. "And now I feel more like shenanigans than ever."

"Oh yeah?" Victoria teased, slowly tracing her fingertips up Mara's arms. "Show me."

"Oh, I will," Mara whispered, her breath warm against Victoria's neck.

Victoria let out a low, guttural moan as her lips caressed the sensitive skin below her jawline. Her knees, already weak with the anticipation of what was to come, buckled as she hit the couch, and she fell backward onto the cushions.

Mara landed on top of her in push-up position, grinding her hips against Victoria, not missing a beat. "Are you getting the picture yet?" She didn't wait for an answer. Instead she sealed her mouth over Victoria's, pushing her tongue past her lips hungrily.

Heat flushed in Victoria's body, her pussy clenching with want. She slid her hands under the edge of Mara's sports bra, nails digging into skin, pulling that beautiful body against hers. She sighed with pleasure as Mara tugged her scrubs off. All the stress of the workday and worry about getting ready for the fundraiser melted away. Her focus was strictly on Mara's glorious touch. Victoria wiggled her hips and kicked her legs free of the pants and her thong, at the same time finally freeing Mara's breasts from the black bra.

"Tell me what you want." Mara nibbled as she spoke, her words slow and dripping like honey.

Another ripple of excitement moved up Victoria's spine. She couldn't get enough of Mara and couldn't get it fast enough. "I want you naked."

"You first," Mara countered, helping her shimmy out of her top and lacy bra. Her gaze ran down the length of Victoria's body, and her eyes sparkled with appreciation.

Victoria leaned back against the pillow and raked her fingertips across Mara's well-toned abs until they came to rest on the waistband of her shorts. Topless wasn't good enough. She wanted to see all of her gorgeous girlfriend. "Now you. Take these off." She snapped the elastic to emphasize her point.

Mara arched a sexy eyebrow. "You've become bossy! But confidence looks good on you, so I will." She slowly teased her shorts down her tan thighs, past her knees, before finally stepping out of them. She stood still for a moment, naked and confident. She bit her lip, her eyes locked on Victoria's as she climbed back on top of her.

"God, you are beautiful," Victoria moaned, as her nipples brushed against Mara and went hard. She grabbed Mara's toned ass with both hands and gave it a squeeze, eliciting a growl from her girlfriend.

"What do you want now?" Mara bit out the words, her breath ragged. Her fingertips found Victoria's swollen clit and she rubbed slow circles around it.

She shuddered under Mara's touch and she arched into her. "Put your fingers inside me, baby." She gasped for breath as Mara complied, filling her up with slow, controlled strokes. She reached a hand between Mara's legs and slipped easily into her soaked pussy.

Mara rode Victoria's hand while she fucked her, harder and faster as they moved together. Her eyes were closed and her head tipped back. Sweat rose on her forehead, a flush crept up her neck, and she gulped air, but she looked absolutely beautiful.

"Look at me." Victoria fixed her gaze on Mara. Staring into her girlfriend's eyes, Victoria gave in to the dizzy feeling overtaking her brain just as the orgasm rocked her body.

Mara cried out as she tightened around Victoria's fingers, her brown curls bouncing off her shoulders as she struggled to catch her breath. Finally she lowered herself down and rested her head on Victoria's chest.

Victoria ran her hand through Mara's hair, enjoying the calm after the storm as her heartbeat returned to a reasonable rate. She was filled with warm satisfaction and she wanted nothing more than to lay with Mara in her arms forever. She bent down to kiss Mara's head. "That was exactly what I wanted."

CHAPTER TWENTY-NINE

"So that's our show." Mara stood on the little stage in the corner of the café and blinked into the spotlight, pleased with her performance and ready to spend the rest of the night by her girlfriend's side. "Thank you all for coming out tonight and supporting Bark Around The Clock. Your generosity will help so many of our furry, four-legged friends find a home, and that is an excellent thing. Don't forget to come by and see me at the Laffmoor at the Rothmoor, where every time is a great time. I am Mara Antonini and I look forward to seeing you all again soon. Goodnight!"

As the crowd burst into applause, Mara hopped down from the makeshift stage and made a beeline for Victoria, who was waiting with arms open. Victoria looked absolutely stunning in a sapphire blue sheath and sparkly silver heels. Mara's heartbeat sped up as she approached the most beautiful woman in the room.

Victoria kissed her and said, "You were awesome!"

"Aw, shucks. You probably say that to all the comedians you date." Mara smiled and batted her eyes.

Victoria slipped her hand into Mara's and gave it a squeeze. "Well, we'll never know because you are the only one for me."

"I love you, Victoria," Mara said, leaning in for one more kiss.

"Hey, take it easy, you two." Penny approached, the clacking of her designer high heels matching the beat of the music the DJ was spinning. "No PDA's while representing the Rothmoor. The last thing we need is a scandal involving our new headliner."

"Scandal involving me?" Mara rolled her eyes at her best friend's dramatics. "Like anyone gives a damn what I do. I could get butt naked and dance the pachanga and no one would even..."

Her words were drowned out by the shrill ring tone of Penny's phone.

Mara winced. "I swear, that is the loudest thing I have ever heard."

"I have to be able to answer calls. I'm technically working, you know," Penny said, but when she glanced at the screen, her expression darkened. "Crap. I've got to take this. It's the casino."

Mara tried not to eavesdrop even though Penny had chosen to take the call right where they stood instead of walking away for a little privacy. Mara leaned in to kiss Victoria on her cheek. She was so happy to have her girlfriend by her side again. When Victoria smiled back at her, eyes bright and shining, Mara felt the butterflies in her belly that Victoria always inspired. It was the same as the night they first got together, and Mara looked forward to enjoying that sensation for a long time to come. Maybe even forever.

"No!" Penny's rising voice snapped Mara back to the present. "I'll handle it. Yeah. I'll go right now."

Mara raised her eyebrows in concern as Penny poked angrily at her phone, clicking off the call. "You okay?"

"No. I'm not." Penny straightened her posture and tugged her purse up on her shoulder with a huff. "A casino manager's job is never done. Anyway, I gotta go. I'll call you tomorrow. Congratulations on a great show, Mara. You made the Rothmoor proud tonight."

Mara smiled graciously and waved Penny away before slipping her hand back into Victoria's. She felt sorry for Penny having to leave.

"Hey!" Victoria leaned in and gave Mara's cheek a quick kiss. "If you need to go with Penny to help her, you can. I'll just meet you at the house later. You do have your own key, after all."

Mara shook her head. "Believe me, Penny can handle anything that job can throw at her. She doesn't need me to go with her."

"So what do you want to do, babe?" Victoria tipped her head onto Mara's shoulder.

Mara looked around the café. There was still a buzz of activity, despite the late hour. Frankie was playing hostess, smiling, shaking hands, reveling in the successful night. Jenna and Hayleigh were forehead to forehead on the dance floor, swaying in time with the music. Partygoers were still doing their thing as well—mixing, mingling, and finishing off the remaining food. But none of those activities appealed to Mara in the slightest. She only had one woman on her mind and that was just the way she liked it. She slipped her arm around Victoria's waist and pulled her close.

"Let's go home."

Bella Books, Inc.

Women. Books. Even Better Together.

P.O. Box 10543
Tallahassee, FL 32302

Phone: 800-729-4992
www.bellabooks.com